W9-DIM-745

WITHDRAWN

The Nun
and Other Stories

Grabado al acero de B. Maura, 1881

Pedro Ant.º de Alarcon

Engraving of Pedro Antonio de Alarcón. Artist: Bartolomé Maura y Montaner. Photo by Robert M. Fedorchek.

The Nun
and Other Stories

by
Pedro Antonio de Alarcón

Translated from the Spanish by
Robert M. Fedorchek

Introduction by
Stephen Miller

Lewisburg
Bucknell University Press
London: Associated University Presses

Associated University Presses
440 Forsgate Drive
Cranbury, NJ 08512

Associated University Presses
16 Barter Street
London WC1A 2AH, England

Associated University Presses
P.O. Box 338, Port Credit
Mississauga, Ontario
Canada L5G 4L8

The paper used in this publication meets the requirements of the American National Standard for Permanence of Paper for Printed Library Materials Z39.48–1984.

Library of Congress Cataloging-in-Publication Data

Alarcón, Pedro Antonio de, 1833–1891.
    The nun and other stories / by Pedro Antonio de Alarcón; translated from the Spanish by Robert M. Fedorchek; introduction by Stephen Miller.
       p.   cm.
    Includes bibliographical references.
    Contents: The nun—Captain Poison—Moors and Christians—The tall woman.
    ISBN 0–8387–5415–5 (alk. paper)
    1. Fedorchek, Robert M., 1938–. II. Title.
PQ6502.A6 1999
863'.5—dc21

                        98–39220
                          CIP
                          Rev.

PRINTED IN THE UNITED STATES OF AMERICA

For Rev. Victor F. Leeber, SJ
Exemplary Jesuit, exemplary friend

Contents

Translator's Preface

VIRTUALLY all critics agree that Pedro Antonio de Alarcón (1833-91) deserves to be considered one of the best short story writers of nineteenth-century Spanish literature. But I do not believe that it is splitting hairs to say that he also deserves to be called one of nineteenth-century Spain's greatest short story *tellers*, a writer who engages the reader through imagination as well as form. And *The Nun and Other Stories* shows that Alarcón's imagination in short prose fiction thrived at the middle of his writing career ("The Nun," 1868) and at the end of it (*Captain Poison* and "Moors and Christians," 1881, and "The Tall Woman," 1882).

One short novel and three short stories, all of which have been translated into English before. Well might the reader ask: Why are these four selections being brought out in a new translation? Apart from their intrinsic worth, always the paramount concern, and aside from the purely practical consideration that the extant translations all went out of print decades ago, only Martin Nozick's "The Nun" is faithful to the original; the other three are sometimes painfully literal, suffer from misinterpretation, and contain sentences— occasionally whole paragraphs—not to be found anywhere in the original. And these original texts have generated much commentary.

José F. Montesinos, along with other well-known critics like Emilia Pardo Bazán, Mariano Baquero Goyanes, and Laura de los Ríos, considers *The Nun* one of the best short stories written in nineteenth-century Spain and calls it "one of Alarcón's rare absolute successes" [uno de los raros aciertos absolutos de Alarcón] (148). Azorín goes even further and says: "And no one has been able to condense in fifteen pages

9

all the psychological history in Spain like Alarcón in *The Nun*"
[Y nadie ha sabido condensar en quince páginas toda la
historia psicológica en España como Alarcón en *La comendadora*] (968). Cyrus DeCoster, author of the only book-
length study in English of Alarcón's work, has written that
Captain Poison is a "somewhat sentimental love story . . .
told with engaging humor . . . a reversal of the traditional
story of *The Taming of the Shrew*" (118). Carmen Bravo-
Villasante writes that it is a work in which Alarcón has given
"free rein to his humorist vein and his tendency to ironic
idealization" [rienda suelta a su vena humorística y a su ten-
dencia de idealización irónica] (11). This short novel enjoyed
great success with the Spanish-reading public when
published in 1881 and deserves to be brought again to the
attention of an English-reading public. Juan Luis Alborg calls
"Moors and Christians," also highly praised by Montesinos
(165–66), "one of the most delightful and amusing tales to
come from Alarcón's pen" [uno de los más sabrosos y diver-
tidos relatos salidos de la pluma de Alarcón] (525). And Laura
de los Ríos, in her edition of selected stories by Alarcón,
devotes ten full pages to an analysis of "The Tall Woman"
(77–86), a fantastic tale that has also been singled out as
among his very best by Azorín and Mariano Baquero
Goyanes.

Recognized critics—Alarcón's contemporaries and ours—
attest to the artistic worth of the selections that make up *The
Nun and Other Stories*, tales which themselves attest to Alarcón's standing in nineteenth-century Spanish short prose
fiction.

Words and passages marked with an asterisk (*) in the text
are explained in the notes section at the back of the book.

Works Cited

Alborg, Juan Luis. *Historia de la literatura española. Realismo y naturalismo. La novela, parte primera: introducción-Fernán Caballero-Alarcón-Pereda.* Madrid: Editorial Gredos, 1996.

Azorín. *Obras selectas.* Madrid: Biblioteca Nueva, 1962.

Bravo-Villasante, Carmen, ed. *La mujer alta y El Capitán Veneno,* by Pedro Antonio de Alarcón. Madrid: Mondadori España, 1988.

De los Ríos, Laura. *La comendadora, El clavo y otros cuentos,* by Pedro Antonio de Alarcón. 8th ed. Madrid: Ediciones Cátedra, 1991.

DeCoster, Cyrus. *Pedro Antonio de Alarcón.* Boston: Twayne Publishers, 1979.

Montesinos, José F. *Pedro Antonio de Alarcón.* Madrid: Editorial Castalia, 1977.

Introduction

TOGETHER with Pérez Galdós, Alas, Pardo Bazán, Palacio Valdés, Pereda, Valera, and Fernán Caballero, Pedro Antonio de Alarcón figures among the major authors of Spanish nineteenth-century narrative. Nonetheless, as viewed by critics contemporary to him and to us, those of his works which are praised—for example "El clavo" [The Nail], "La Comendadora" [The Nun], El sombrero de tres picos [The Three-Cornered Hat], and El Capitán Veneno [Captain Poison]—primarily exhibit, according to those critics, traditional story-telling values. But such values are not associated with the polysemic, self-referential, and hermetic modes of fiction most valued by critics. Alarcón's works which are fiercely denigrated—El escándalo [The Scandal], El Niño de la bola [The Infant with the Globe], and La pródiga [The Prodigal Woman]—offend because of their alleged conservative and even reactionary ideology. In practice, this situation leaves us with an author many of whose productions please when read—as may be seen in translator Robert M. Fedorchek's selection in this volume as well as in that of his previous "The Nail" and Other Stories—but whose work occupies a less than strong position in that list of must-read titles we call the canon.

In what follows I shall rehearse briefly the literary career of Alarcón and the reception that critics from his times to the present afford it. Then I shall describe an Alarcón, clearly viewable in the present volume, who seems to have eluded the attention of critics both favorable and unfavorable to his work as a whole. It is an Alarcón who explains and justifies a rate of continued translation from his times to the present far in excess of what his standing among critics would lead an observer to expect. And it is an Alarcón whose claim to our attention may be surprisingly timely in the context of the contemporary crisis of Spanish nationalism.

The most important primary source of information about Alarcón continues to be his own writing, especially the 1884 general prologue to the first edition of his complete works. "Historia de mis libros" [History of My Books] synthesizes elements of Alarcón's personal biography with details about the genesis, publication, and reception of his books. As many critics have commented, the "History" is also an apology for Alarcón's creations and his aesthetics, especially from the avowed perspective of a man who views himself at age fifty-one as old and who will write no more fiction. Other important autobiographical sources about the author are found in his reportorial books and in his articles and occasional writings and discourses about literature and morality.

In "History of My Books," Alarcón divides his literary life into two distinct epochs separated by the 1862–73 interim period of direct political activity. The first epoch begins in the very early 1850s with the romantic verse and prose Alarcón publishes first in newspapers and then in book form, and concludes with the volumes of reportage and travel that consecrate him as a national figure and leave him financially independent: *Diario de un testigo de la Guerra de Africa* [*Diary of a Witness to the War in Africa* (1860)] and *De Madrid a Nápoles* [*From Madrid to Naples* (1861)]. In this epoch, Alarcón's only dramatic work to achieve commercial production is poorly received, and he writes the great majority of his short narratives. It is also the period when, according to "The History of My Books," Alarcón lives and writes most under the influence of "la sublime pero enervante poesia de lord Byron" [the sublime but enervating poetry of Lord Byron].

This youthful Alarcón is a noncontroversial literary figure whose claim to fame today would be as an author included in anthologies of the Spanish short story of the nineteenth century. Historians would also value this Alarcón because the *Diary of a Witness to the War in Africa*, illustrated with woodcuts based on photographs and drawings by artists in the field, is a fundamental primary source of images, facts, impressions, and opinions of the Spanish-Moroccan war from December 1859 to March 1860.

Alarcón's second epoch is more complex, richer, more polemical, and, from my viewpoint, more poorly understood by critics. It begins with his third travel book, *La Alpujarra* [*The Alpujarra* (1873)]. This volume establishes a continuity in Alarcón's literary career by completing the author's travel-book trilogy initiated by the 1860 and 1861 titles, the last major productions of his first epoch. Furthermore, following a decade of political activity, *The Alpujarra* reintroduces him to the public as the already well-known and admired literary figure. Although Alarcón creates several of his best short stories during this second period, it is the 1881 and 1882 publication of three volumes of his collected but mostly earlier-written stories that consolidates his ranking as an important author in the genre. Moreover, it is the publication of *The Three-Cornered Hat* in 1874, *The Scandal* the following year, and the 1877 "Discourse on Morality in Art" that places Alarcón in the first rank of Spanish novelists of his time while simultaneously making him the center of fierce polemics involving literature, politics, religion, and morality. For all practical purposes this second epoch concludes in 1884, some seven years before the author's death, with the already mentioned "History of My Books." Therein he refers to the "History" as his literary "testament" and recalls his purpose, stated two years before in the dedication to *The Prodigal Woman*, to write no more new books. The novels *The Infant with the Globe* (1880) and *Captain Poison* (1881) round out the major production of the second epoch.

To judge by both critical opinion and the number of new editions and translations, *The Three-Corned Hat* is Alarcón's masterpiece. I would affirm that many of his short stories as well as all of his novels share the positive attributes signaled by critics of *The Three-Cornered Hat*: a solid story line; well-drawn characters and settings; and, most especially, lively narration. While critics rank and judge differently Alarcón's three travel narratives, the books share to the extent compatible with reportorial creation the virtues of their author's best fiction, and add to them accurate, informed views of contemporary customs, characters, and conflicts. In *Diary of a Witness to the War in Africa*, Alarcón studies and describes Moroccans, North African Jews, and Spanish officers and soldiers in the context of the invasion of the Spanish army in 1859–60. *From Madrid to Naples* sketches aspects of Second Empire France under Napoleon III at his zenith and the remote quiet of the Alps—the prosperity of Switzerland, the squalor of the recently contested Savoy— but concentrates on the divided Italy of the Risorgimento and the formation of the Kingdom of Italy. *The Alpujarra* considers the past and present of the author's native Alpujarra region in Andalusia. Comprising mountainous parts of the provinces of Granada and Almeria, the region was a Moorish stronghold on the Iberian Peninsula until the eve of the discovery of America, and Alarcón is at pains to plead the virtues of tolerance and to stress the singularity of the Alpujarra's Moorish heritage enduring in its Christian present.

The critical complaint about Alarcón centers on three of his second-epoch novels—*The Scandal, The Infant with the Globe*, and *The Prodigal Woman*—and on his 1877 discourse upon entering the Spanish Royal Academy of the Language. The complete charge against these works is that not only do they reveal their author to be an extreme Spanish ultramontanist, they demonstrate a religiously and philosophically conservative apologetics of a kind not suited to fictive exposition. A complementary defect is, according to these critics, that Alarcón reveals also a lack of academic sophistication, which makes his arguments less than they might have been if formulated by a person of greater education. The dominant tone of critical reaction, from the 1875–77 period of *The Scandal* and the academic discourse onwards, could be characterized by such words as surprise, offense, and condescension. From the critics' viewpoint, Alarcón persists in his errors in two of his last three novels, and critics of his time and since answer by not commenting on them, or, in the best of cases, by loosely adapting to them negative comments evoked by their detailed censure of *The Scandal*. Even when such influential contemporaries of Alarcón such as Revilla, Alas, Valera, and Pardo Bazán urge Alarcón to return and add to the aesthetics of *The Three-Cornered Hat*, an affronted Alarcón rejoins by announcing he will write no more. He takes cognizance only of what offends him in their criticism: their ideologically and/or aesthetically oriented condemnation of what they consider unfortunate tendencies in all his second-epoch major works following *The Three-Cornered Hat* and excepting only *Captain Poison*. In addition, and this becomes a new motive for censure, critics of then and now detect in Alarcón's reactions to criticism from the middle 1870s onward an overweening pride (*soberbia*) that enjoys a "me-against-them-all" position in the panorama of Spanish letters.

In my judgment, both Alarcón and his critics overemphasize the polemical dimensions to his work. Whatever errors Alarcón may have committed because of pride, belief, or judgment, he died more than a century ago, and it is the work that remains. No matter how powerful the sectarian passions those issues inflamed then, by now most readers neither understand nor care about the Jesuits and ultramontanism in the last third of the nineteenth century. Furthermore, with the establishment of a true Spanish democracy following the death of Franco in 1975 and now a generation old, it is time for critics to make an adaption analogous to that of Spanish society in political matters: approach Alarcón from a contemporary perspective. In practice this means the abandonment of the ideological battle of the two Spains that commences in the early nineteenth century when Bourbon, aristocratic, and ecclesiastic absolutism is first rejected by nascent, Spanish, democratic liberalism. But this kind of change is proving more difficult in intellectual circles than in the larger society. In a way especially characteristic of Spain, where Alarcón followed many others in going from literature directly into politics, and where today cultural concerns still occupy more public attention than is common in the world, the opinions and writings of a major author easily become an essential factor in national and regional discussion and debate. And once the characterization of a writer as liberal, conservative, or apolitical forms, it remains fixed, sometimes regardless of its accuracy.

During restoration of the Bourbon monarchy beginning in 1874, and following six years of unsuccessful experiments with democracy in which Alarcón participated, *The Scandal* and the 1877 academic discourse were very socially and politically relevant. By virtue of giving prominence, not pre-eminence, to conservative religious and ethical thematics in those works, Alarcón entered into the highly charged political wars between those who viewed themselves either as effectively vanquished liberals or triumphant conservatives. His position was aggravated by his shift from participation in the experiments in democracy to support for the restoration. Hence, when Alarcón portrayed positive aspects of the Jesuits and the church in *The Scandal* and later in *The Infant with the Globe*, or showed middle-class politicians in a negative way in *The Prodigal Woman*, liberals were upset. Even critics such as Valera were provoked on nonpolitical grounds because it seemed that Alarcón was adulterating aesthetics with ideology. His pride piqued, Alarcón stopped writing and acerbated the situation by letting one polemical facet of his work come to represent all of it. By creating no more new works that, like *The Three-Corned Hat* and *Captain Poison*, might have shown a nonpolemical Alarcón, the author deprived himself and readers of the possibility of sharing the perspectives and insights of a major author as he reacted to his times through new fictions and, maybe, travel books. But the silent Alarcón helped to pigeonhole himself in a way that, from the other side of the political spectrum, Pérez Galdós would have done had he ceased writing after his controversially liberal ideological novels of the 1870s: *Doña Perfecta, Gloria, La familia de León Roch* [*The Family of Leon Roch*]. By continuing to create, as did the prolific Galdós, Alarcón would have made it more difficult to caricature his work and have the caricature stand for the whole. Response to both new and old works by him would have become more complex, more complete.

In my reading of criticism on Alarcón, the most notable aspect of the centenary of his death in 1991 is the extent to which most publications designed to mark that date break no new ground in Alarconian studies. Furthermore, in my opinion, by simply rehashing critical commonplaces engendered by the two-Spains ideological debate of Alarcón's time, such publications leave their readers with the implicit question of why anyone would want to read Alarcón. But events have moved quickly between 1991 and now. So much so that the old ideological clichés as applied to Alarcón have, in my opinion, become obviously and conclusively irrelevant. During the entire post-Franco period, the issue of what constitutes Spain has been assuming greater importance. Concretely this means that the Imperial and Francoist vision of a highly centralized, Spanish-speaking nation has been under assault by Catalonians, Basques, Galicians, Canary Islanders, and other regional groupings. But since 1991 this process has gone so far as to bring into question the substantiveness of Spain as a contemporarily relevant concept. In a country where demands for regional autonomy have reached potentially nation-splitting proportions, the question and the ideological relevance of all two-Spains-oriented polemics belong to the past. Hence, because Alarcón's reputation in the critical establishment has remained virtually unchanged since ossifying between 1875 and the author's death, and because inoperative ideological premises have continued to mediate any reading of Alarcón by the critical establishment, significant dimensions of Alarcón have gone unrecognized. In fact, as we shall see, the Andalusian regionalist dimension of Alarcón's work may be, most especially in today's Spain, cause in itself for a serious rereading of Alarcón.

Fedorchek's translations come, then, at a very opportune time: they let us see Alarcón with new eyes. And in what follows, our purpose is to seek out a different, probably richer Alarcón. He is the missing Alarcón, the writer who became a casualty of the long two-Spains war of 170 years between the first Spanish constitution—that of 1812, written in Cadiz—and the consolidation of Spanish democracy by the early 1980s.

The missing Alarcón is the mature realist of the first and second-epoch travel books, the acute, direct observer of regional, national, and international social and political manners and history. The essential principle guiding this writer is probably best expressed in the seventh chapter of the first book of *From Naples to Madrid*. It is formulated when Alarcón realizes that he has already spent a month and a half in Paris, clearly acknowledged by him as the center of the Western world. He characterizes his stay there as a frenzy of meeting and talking with people of all classes, backgrounds, and occupations, and this while seeing as much of Paris and its environs as possible. With something of a Dantean accent, he states:

¡Oh! yo buscaba la verdad en medio de tantas farsas y mentiras; yo buscaba el por qué de las cosas, el objeto, el fin, el ideal de la vida moderna; la fe, la creencia, el interés supremo de la actual civilización; su eje, su polo, su término adorado.

[Oh! I was seeking the truth in the midst of so many farces and lies; I was seeking the why of things, the object, the end, the ideal of modern life; the faith, the belief, the supreme interest of present civilization; its axis, its pole, its adored end.]

In common with many generations of Spaniards, Alarcón sees the French as representing the greatest level of material progress in the world. Yet he mistrusts their civilization and the path it signals to the rest of the world. Now, on the eve of his travels through Switzerland and the Savoy into a troubled Italian Peninsula, Alarcón already is a seasoned observer of cultural variety, difference, and value. The traditions and customs of his native Alpujarra region of abiding Moorish folkways contrast strongly with Madrid. Whereas the historic mission of Madrid is to be the melting pot of Spain, the country, as is especially evident today, is one where the use of "Castilian" as an adjective always reminds everyone of the great regional differences of languages, peoples, and historical experience which constitute Iberia. Galicians, Basques, Catalonians, Andalusians, not to mention the Portuguese, all have traditional reasons for viewing Castile with suspicion and for not accepting fully the idea of Spain. To this experience, and before *From Madrid to Naples*, the author of *Diary*

of a Witness to the War of Africa adds the bloody violence of
warring national armies of tens of thousands of soldiers, as
well as the calmer observations of cultural difference by
coming to know Islamic and Jewish Moroccans during the
Spanish occupation of Tetuán. Moreover, Alarcón understands the complexities and dark side of his nation's politics:
following the taking of Tetuán, a jingoistic public back home
wants an extended war of conquest and land acquisition
while officers and soldiers in the field know that all initial
objectives are secured and the new ones are neither just nor
easily obtained.

Bearing in mind this well-known but little-frequented
province of Alarcón's literary production, it should not be
surprising that there is more to *The Three-Cornered Hat* than
the amusing tale of an old goat's lust being foiled and
punished by his would-be victim's virtue and intelligence.
Figured in the personages of the novel, set in the last, uncon-
tested days of Spanish absolutism (1804–8) and in the
author's home town of Guadix, is a study of the structure
and abuse of power: of the mistrust and suffering that those
officially charged with upholding and administering the social
order cause when they have no honor and use their position
to trample the dignity and virtue of those over whom they
have sway.

For its part, and not unlike *The Three-Cornered Hat* in this
specific regard, *The Scandal* is also more complex than the
usual, ideologically conditioned perceptions of it would
recognize. It is common to read the novel as an apology for a
religiously based moral order represented by the old Jesuit
Father Manrique's prescriptions for the salvation of the
noble, notorious, Byronic Fabián Conde. Missing, though,
from such readings are two extremely significant dimensions: the novel's personally and culturally important critique
of the Byronism that always fascinated Alarcón, and its
exploration of the areligious, Senecan stoicism embodied in
Fabián's misunderstood, wronged, long-suffering friend
Lázaro. For *The Scandal* is indeed a kind of literary, rhetori-
cally balanced *disputatio* embodied in the opposing positions
and conflicts of the characters. The Jesuit Manrique's Chris-

tian analysis of Conde's ills and his recommendations to correct them are strongly formulated. But what makes them literarily effective is not their orthodoxy but their part in revealing the panorama of passions, reasons, needs and limitations of the human condition, particularly as the reader compares and contrasts them with the virtuous paganism of Lázaro's Iberian stoicism and the dramatic willfulness of Conde's Byronism. Further diversity of character and moral views are incarnated in Conde's other friend, the hot-headed, unreasoning, unhappily married Diego. And the gallery of secondary personages, composed mainly of a morally and socially heterogeneous group of blood or political relatives of those already mentioned, adds further pertinent comparisons and contrasts to Alarcón's fiction about the complexity of moral action and our need to come to terms with what we want balanced by what we can have.

In this developing context of Alarconian literature, I think it clear that the customarily condescending dismissal of the academic "Discourse on Morality in Art" is temerarious. Alarcón's rehearsal of the history of the relation of the True, the Good, and the Beautiful openly dialogues with a main current of Western thought from the ancient Greeks to our time. When Alarcón questions any art that claims to be beautiful without at the same time putting into play the claims of truth and goodness, his reasoning is not *in its type* different from Plato's discussion of the poets in the *Republic*. Whatever Alarcón's, or Plato's, unpopular conclusions, the issues raised are foundational in our civilization.

The same kind of incomplete, ideological reading that has stood between generations of readers and *The Scandal* has had a version applicable to *The Infant with the Globe*. It draws parallels between two exemplary priests, Fathers Manrique and Muley, and the two erring young men they would guide: Fabián Conde and Manuel Venegas, the eponymous "Infant with the Globe." Yet, just as the tendentious emphasis on the Manrique-Conde relation leads to an incomplete reading of *The Scandal*, so too does undue stress on the Muley-Venegas pairing produce a decentering of the conflicts of *The Infant with the Globe*. When Conde finds

himself checked in his desires to marry Gabriela, and
Venegas in his to wed Soledad, Fathers Manrique and Muley
supply their respective charges with religiously based,
difficult-to-follow, moral courses of action. Were the acceptance or rejection of the priests' counsel the only source of
the two protagonists' moral dilemmas and choices, the two
novels would justify tendentious interpretations and consequent critical censure. Clearly, though, this is not the case
with *The Scandal*, nor, I think, with *The Infant with the
Globe*. As Alarcón often did in seeking fictional materials, for
the main story line of this latter title he relied on oral tales
known to him from his native Guadix in the Alpujarra. The
case of *The Infant with the Globe* is noteworthy. Like *The
Three-Cornered Hat*, it is set in Guadix, but in a much more
radical way. Events of *The Three-Cornered Hat* transpired
more than twenty-five years before Alarcón's birth and
among persons not native to the Alpujarra. But in his "The
History of My Books," Alarcón relates that *The Infant with
the Globe*, especially its culminating actions, is a "*drama
romántico*" that he himself witnessed in the Gaudix of his
childhood. Beginning in the first paragraph of this "romantic
drama" in novel form, Alarcón announces the theme that
counterbalances throughout the book Muley's unwavering
Catholic thought and action, particularly in relation to his
attempt to guide Venegas: that in that town and region "hay
todavía muchos moros vestidos de cristianos" [there are still
many Moors dressed as Christians]. In a simple but telling
way, Father Trinidad Muley's names intensify the theme of
the divided cultural and religious allegiances that the people
of Guadix and all the Alpujarra live: the priest's first name,
Trinidad [Trinity], could hardly be more emblematically
Christian, and his family name, Muley, is obviously Moorish.
Moreover, Manuel Venegas's father, we learn, took pride in
descending from a Moorish prince who could trace his
ancestry to the prophet Mohammed! And when Manuel
himself prepares to confront the man who, in Manuel's long,
obligatory absence, took Soledad from him, we read, where
the reference is to Manuel: "Los moros son siempre
vanidosos y artistas, y acuden a las batallas con sus mejores

ropas y todo el posible boato, viendo tal vez una fiesta en el peligro" [The Moors are always vain and artistic, and present themselves in battle with their best clothes and all possible ornamentation, seeing perhaps a holiday in the danger]. Hence, the true conflict of *The Infant with the Globe* has little to do with the ideological turmoil of the years following restoration of the Bourbons to the Spanish throne. As befits the author of the three travel books in which cultural, regional, and national traditions and values are observed and analyzed, this novel explores the unresolved conflict between the avowed principles guiding the society from which Alarcón arose, and the perhaps more powerful inherited instincts from an earlier, pre-Christian time.

Alarcón's final fiction is the novel *The Prodigal Woman.* It is possible that critics cite more frequently the comment from the dedicatory respecting it being his last novel than they comment on the novel itself. Hence it is not surprising that even when the subgenre of the aristocratic novel, the realistic portrayal of the highest level of Spanish society, is being discussed in versions as written, with more or less success, by such colleagues of Alarcón as Pereda, Pardo Bazán, Palacio Valdés, and Coloma, *The Prodigal Woman* is overlooked. This is especially ironic because the novel centers upon a still attractive marquise in her late thirties who has been forgotten by the world.

The marquise Julia is the last member of her family, grandees of the old landed aristocracy. After spending her fortune across Europe in her days of glory, she retires to her last remaining possession. With just enough income to support her and served by faithful peasants from the old days, she lives completely apart from the great world in which she shined brilliantly. The novel begins during an election campaign in the mid 1860s. Three political hopefuls, in their early twenties and forming part of the still-emerging Spanish middle class based in Madrid, travel through southern Spain in search of votes. They meet the marquise Julia because even in her diminished state she remains the politically most influential person in the district. One of the three, Guillermo, becomes attracted to the marquise and she to him. Following a protracted attempt to reject a love she recognizes as impractical and potentially hurtful to her, she receives him. As happens in *The Scandal*, Alarcón masterfully orchestrates a second fictive *disputatio*. By creating a clear, dramatic structure of exposition, complication, and resolution, the reasoning of Julia and Guillermo about their situations and conflicts, and the reactions of their respective friends and acquaintances to the stages of their decision making, come alive. Whatever the morality of the reader, the center of the novel is the process of moral decision in the face of immediate human need. Furthermore, the intensity of the protagonists' struggle is increased by the issues of secular social change that Alarcón has woven into the story. In this case, Julia and Guillermo are not simply a woman and a man. She is an aristocrat of blood and principle who understands her errors and freely accepts her exile from the great world; he is a talented, ambitious, middle-class man in the process of making a self and a society in which improvisation and expediency dominate. Their conversations and letters, and the societally imposed costs of their relationship, figure the passage from an old, ideal Spain of reckless but real honor to an inexperienced, opportunistic, new Spain whose virtues are yet to be discovered. While the old Spain knows what is being lost and must accept the new situation as the price for having any life, the new Spain is much less conscious of its position. It has neither a living memory of the values of the past nor a vision of the future which takes into account the strengths and weaknesses of the past. Perhaps Alarcón, who came from a good family fallen on hard times, in some way represented himself, who once used the pen name *El hijo pródigo* [The prodigal son], in the marquise, and in the society that rejects the Julia-Guillermo pairing, the literary establishment that did not understand him and from which he took leave in the dedicatory to the novel.

Fedorchek's selection from Alarcón for the present volume includes what I call the missing Alarcón, represented by *Captain Poison*, as well as three of the author's praised short stories. As is the case with *The Three-Cornered Hat*, the novel of Captain Poison and Angustias has always been considered a good book and a nonpolemical creation. On this level it is seen as a Spanish, nineteenth-century version of *The Taming of the Shrew*, but offering an amusing innovation: the gender roles are reversed, as a serious, attractive, young woman tames a crusty military man of forty who prefers battles and jungles to society and cities, the rigors of campaigning to the company of women. Yet *Captain Poison* is also more. It explores how Angustias comes to recognize in Captain Poison the qualities she most valued in her dead father, a valiant and noble Carlist general; how the death of Captain Poison's mother in childbirth and the consequent suicide of his distraught father distanced him from the ways of family and society; and how Angustias leads the captain to embrace life and create with her the family she lost and he never knew.

One of the recurring motifs of Alarcón's fiction, inspired probably by his wide, youthful reading in romanticism, is the orphan. Limiting ourselves to characters in works considered here, Captain Poison and Angustias, Fabián Conde, Lázaro, and Diego from *The Scandal,* and Manuel Venegas from *The Infant with the Globe* are prominent Alarconian orphans. The problem they all share, but do not equally well resolve, is to make good their lives not only without the benefit of guiding parents but sometimes needing also to avoid or correct those persons' errors. Two of the three stories translated here by Fedorchek strike me as curiously relevant to the dilemmas of these orphans. In "The Nun," the protagonist's mother chooses to disregard her husband's last will and testament, and in so doing puts into motion the process leading to what he most feared: the extinction of his family line. "Moors and Christians" is more exotic in that a series of Christians and Moors try to controvert the four-hundred-year-old will of an Alpujarran Moor; but the result is not dissimilar to that in "The Nun": violation of the provisions of the will lead to the death of all who take part in that action. What this motif and that of the orphan have in common is their reflection on generational relations and forces. This theme is, of course, a primary social concern in the 1870s through 1880s Spain that is disputing democratic versus

monarchic forms of government, open inquiry versus ecclesiastic dogmatism.

While critics of the past and present have, with Alarcón's
help, as we have seen, pigeonholed him as a doctrinaire
conservative, our reading of Alarcón, now specifically reinforced by the ambiguities of the motifs of the orphan and the
violated will, rejects that position. Further support for this
new view of Alarcón may be found in the third story by him
translated for this volume by Fedorchek. "The Tall Woman,"
a late second-epoch creation dating from August 1881, is a
story whose action passes in the Madrid of the mid 1870s.
But it is narrated in the heights of the Guadarrama Mountains, on the border between the provinces of Madrid and
the Segovia of the famous Roman aqueduct, and several
miles away from a famous symbol of Spanish Catholic Imperial absolutism: the severe palace/monastery of Philip II
called El Escorial. Gabriel, the narrator, is a naturalist, as
are three of his listeners; a painter and a writer round out
the group. In the last two paragraphs of "The Tall Woman,"
we learn that what we are reading is that writer's recounting
of Gabriel's narration. And the writer makes Gabriel's unanswered question to his listeners the question he in his turn
leaves for his readers to answer: whether to believe that a
series of strange encounters by the protagonist of Gabriel's
narration, the engineer Telesforo, and then by Gabriel
himself, were of a supernatural nature. This open-ended
story about the relations between this world and the next,
told in borderlands between ancient Rome and dogmatic
Spain, pondered by nineteenth-century scientists and
artists, and offering to very late twentieth-century readers a
version of doubts we also have is not, I submit, the kind of
story a doctrinaire religious conservative would write and
publish near career's end. It is time to read Pedro Antonio de
Alarcón anew, and Robert M. Fedorchek's translations here
and in *"The Nail" and Other Stories* are fine places to begin.

—Stephen Miller

Caricature of Pedro Antonio de Alarcón by Angel Pons on the cover of the 13 October 1888 issue of *Los Madriles*. Photo by Robert M. Fedorchek. Courtesy, Hemeroteca Municipal, Madrid.

Pedro Antonio de Alarcón in Emilia Pardo Bazán's
Alarcón: estudio biográfico. Photo by Michael A.
Micinilio.

The Nun
and Other Stories

The Nun

The Story of a Woman Who Had No Love Life

I

AROUND eleven o'clock on a March morning nearly one hundred years ago, the sun appeared as cheerful and benign as it is now at the beginning of spring 1868, and as it will be for our great-grandchildren in another century (provided the world has not ended by then); it shone through the balconies of the main salon of a great manor house located on the Carrera de Darro* in Granada, bathing with its brilliant light and pleasant warmth that vast and lordly room, giving life to the religious paintings that covered the walls, rejuvenating the ancient furniture and faded tapestries, and taking the place of the abolished brazier for three people, alive and important at the time, but of whom today there barely remains any trace or memory.

Near a balcony sat a venerable old woman whose noble and energetic face, which had probably once been very beautiful, betrayed an inordinate pride and the most austere virtue. Certainly that mouth had never smiled, and the hard creases at her lips stemmed from the habit of giving orders. Her tremulous head could only have been bowed before altars, and her eyes seemed to flash with the thunderbolt of excommunication. Shortly after looking at that woman, one knew that wherever she wielded power there would be no other choice but to obey her or kill her. Nevertheless, the

33

expression on her face revealed neither cruelty nor evil intent, rather narrowness of principles and an intolerance of behavior that made her incapable of compromising with anything or anyone.

This lady wore a skirt and waist of black worsted like the queen's, and covered her meager gray hair with a shawl of yellowish Belgian lace. On her lap she held an open prayer book, but her eyes had strayed from it to watch a little boy of six or seven who was playing and talking to himself as he rolled on the carpet in one of the rectangles of sunlight that the balconies projected on the floor of the spacious room.

This little boy was frail, pale, blond, and sickly, like the children of Philip IV painted by Velázquez.* A network of purplish veins and big, blue, protuberant eyes stood out prominently on his large head; and, like all rachitic children, he displayed an extraordinarily lively imagination and a certain troublesome irascibility, inasmuch as he was always at the ready to bid defiance. Like a little man, he wore black silk stockings, shoes with buckles, blue satin breeches, a colorfully embroidered waistcoat of the same material, and a long, black velvet frock coat.

At the moment he was amusing himself by tearing the pages out of a beautiful book of heraldry and ripping them into tiny pieces with his emaciated fingers, all the while engaged in disagreeable, unbearable, incoherent chatter, the main import of which was, "Tomorrow I'm going to do this. Today I'm not going to do that. I want such a thing. I don't want such a thing," as if his aim were to challenge the intolerance and censure of the terrible old woman.

The poor child also inspired terror!

Finally, in a corner of the salon (from which she could see the sky, the tops of a few trees, and the reddish towers of the Alhambra, but where she could not *be* seen except by the birds that circled over the Darro River), there sat in a straight-backed chair, motionless, with her gaze lost in the infinite blue of the atmosphere and slowly fingering the amber beads of a very long rosary, a nun, or, to be more exact, a *comendadora*, a religieuse of the Order of Saint James,* about thirty years old, and dressed in the somewhat secular garb usually worn by these ladies in their cells. This garb consisted of black cordovan, high-fronted shoes, a serge skirt and bodice, also black, and a wide, linen shawl fastened to her shoulders with pins, not in a triangular form as with laywomen, but with the two corners of one side gathered together in front and the other two hanging down her back. This arrangement left the lower part of the nun's bodice uncovered, and the red cross of the Holy Apostle* stood out on the left side. She wore neither the white cloak nor the wimple, and, thanks to the absence of the latter, her abundant black hair glistened, all of it combed upward and gathered at the back in that kind of bow that Andalusian peasant women call a *castaña*, like a sort of bun.

Despite the drawbacks of such attire, she was still a strikingly beautiful woman, or, rather, her very beauty was much indebted to the artless dress that allowed her natural feminine pulchritude to stand out more freely. The *comendadora* was tall, robust, slim, and well proportioned, like that noble caryatid that people admire at the entrance to the sculpture galleries of the Vatican. Her woolen clothes clung to her body and revealed, more than covered, the classical form and exquisite beauty of her splendid figure. Her matte white hands were slender, dimpled, and transparent, and stood out bewitchingly over the black skirt, calling to mind those hands of ancient marble, sculpted by Greek chisels, that have been found in Pompeii near the statues to which they belonged.

In order to complete this majestic figure, imagine a dark face, somewhat wasted (or, rather, somewhat etched by the burin of feeling), oval-shaped like Titian's Magdalene,* and suffused with a profound, almost yellowy, pallor, and made much more interesting (since any suggestion of insensitivity was removed) by two deep, purplish rings under her eyes, rings full of mysterious sadness that were a kind of twilight of the stricken suns of her eyes. Those eyes, almost always cast downward, rose only to look up at heaven, as if they did not dare to settle on the things of this world. When she lowered them, it seemed that their long lashes became the shadows of eternal night, falling over a purposeless, ill-fated existence; and when she raised them, it seemed that her heart was escaping through them on a luminous cloud in order to become as one with the bosom of the Creator. But if by chance they rested on some earthly creature or thing, then those jet-black eyes would blaze, trembling and wandering, utterly terrified, as if they were inflamed by fever or were going to be flooded with tears.

Imagine too a clear, haughty brow, thick eyebrows with a sober, noble outline, the most well-formed and artistic of noses, and a provocative, affectionate, divine mouth, and you will form an idea of that enchanting woman who combined at once all the charms of pagan beauty and all the mystical loveliness of Christian heroines.

II

WHAT family was this that we have just resurrected to the light of the sun that set a hundred years ago? Let us quickly give an account of it.

The elderly woman was the widowed Countess of Santos, who, by her marriage to the seventh count of this title, had two children, one son and one daughter, who lost their father at an early age.

But let us go back a little further.

The House of Santos had amassed great wealth and power in the lifetime of the countess's father-in-law, but as that gentleman had only one son and there existed no collateral branches, he began to fear that his family line might disappear, and he stipulated the following in his will (upon establishing new entailments with the favors he had obtained from Philip V during the War of Succession*): "If my heir should have more than one child, he shall divide the property between the two oldest, so that my name, with the blood of my veins, can be propagated worthily in two branches."

Now then, that clause would have had to have been executed in his two grandchildren, that is, in the two children of the severe old woman with whom we have just become acquainted. But, believing that the luster of a family name is much better preserved in a single, powerful branch than in two diluted ones, she determined of her own accord, so as to reconcile her ideas with the wishes of the founder, to have her daughter renounce, if not life, all earthly possessions and take the nun's habit, by which means the whole of the House of Santos would be the exclusive patrimony of her other child, who, by virtue of being firstborn and male, constituted his aristocratic mother's pride and joy.

Thus, when her unfortunate daughter, the second child of the Count of Santos, was barely eight years old, she was shut up in the convent of the *comendadoras* of the Order of Saint James and called Doña Isabel so that she might acclimate herself immediately to monastic life, which was her inescapable fate.

The little girl grew up there, breathing only the air of the cloister and never being consulted about her own inclinations until, having reached that station in life when all rational beings lay out the paths of their future in the field of fantasy, she took the veil of Christ's bride with the indifferent meekness of one who did not even imagine the right or possibility of having a say on her own behalf. There is more: as Doña Isabel could not grasp at that time the full significance of the vows that she had just taken (so ignorant was she still of what the world was and what the human heart embraced) yet could, on the other hand, discern perfectly (since she too was proud of her noble descent) the great advantages that her profession would bring to the splendor of her name, it turned out that she became a nun with a certain self-satisfaction, but not open, outright joy.

But the years went by quickly, and Sister Isabel, who had grown up feeble and frail and who at the time of her profession was, if not a child, an underdeveloped, late-blooming woman, all of a sudden displayed the luxurious nature and extraordinary beauty that we have already admired and whose charms were nothing compared to the splendid springtime that bloomed simultaneously in her heart and soul. From that day forward the young *comendadora* was the wonder and idol of the community as well as of everyone who entered that convent whose rule is very lenient, like all the others of their order. Some compared Sister Isabel with Rebecca, some with Sarah, some with Ruth, and others with Judith. The man who tuned the organ called her Saint Cecilia; the almoner, Saint Paula; the sacristan, Saint Monica. In other words, jointly they attributed to her a considerable resemblance to married, widowed, and spinster saints.

Sister Isabel looked more than once through the Bible and the *Flos Sanctorum** to read the stories of those heroines, those queens, those wives, those materfamilias with whom she found herself compared, and, as a result of such stories, vanity, ambition, and curiosity about life beyond the convent took root in her imagination with so much force that her spiritual director was obliged to reproach her severely, saying that "the direction that her ideas and feelings were taking was the one most calculated to end up in eternal damnation."

The reaction produced in Sister Isabel when she heard these words was at once instantaneous, absolute, and final. From that day forward people saw only a haughty young noblewoman infatuated with her lineage, and a devout, mystical virgin of the Lord who was fervent to the point of ecstasy and delirium, who engaged in such extremes of mortification and entertained such subtle scruples that the superior and her own mother had to admonish her a number of times, not to mention her confessor, who, besides not seeing anything from which to absolve her, would also try to calm her.

What became, meanwhile, of the *comendadora's* heart and soul, that heart and that soul whose sudden flowering was so exuberant?

No one can say for sure.

It is only known that after five years (during which time her brother married, had a son, and became a widower), Sister Isabel, more beautiful than ever, but languid like a fading lily, was moved from the convent to her home, on the advice of doctors and thanks to the influence of her mother, so that she might breathe there the salutary air of the Carrera de Darro, the only cure that they had hit upon for the mysterious ailment that was destroying her life. Some called this ailment "excessive religious zeal," and others called it "dark melancholy," but the only certainty was that it could not be classified among physical illnesses except by its symptoms, which were extreme languor and a continuous propensity to tears.

The removal to her home brought back her health and strength, if not her happiness. But, since her brother Alfonso died around that time, orphaning his three-year-old son, it was determined that the *comendadora* would stay on indefinitely, with her home as her convent, so that she could accompany her elderly mother and look after her young nephew, the sole and universal heir to the Santos countship.

With the above we also know now who the youngster was who was tearing up the book of heraldry on the carpet, and it only remains for us to say, although it can easily be guessed, that that little boy was the life, soul, love, and pride, while at the same time the fierce tyrant, of his grandmother and aunt, who saw in him not only a distinct person but also the sole hope for the propagation of their line.

III

LET us come back to our three characters now that we know them in and out.

The boy stood up all of a sudden, tossed aside the remains of the book, and left the room singing loudly, in search no doubt of some other object to break to pieces, while the two women remained seated right where we left them a short time ago, except that the elderly countess went back to her interrupted reading and the nun stopped fingering the rosary.

What was the nun thinking about?

Who knows . . . !

Spring had arrived. A few canaries and nightingales, in cages hanging from the balconies outside of the salon, kept up some kind of dialogue with the birds of both sexes that lived freely and happily in the Alhambra's groves, with the hapless captives perhaps relating to them the sadness and boredom typical of all loveless lives. The pots of wallflowers, Virginia stocks, and hyacinths that adorned the balconies were beginning to bloom, a sign that nature was about to bring forth new life once again. The air, perfumed and mild, seemed to beckon lovers from the cities to the pleasant solitude of the countryside, or to the sweet mystery of the forests, where they could look at one another freely and reveal their innermost thoughts. And from the streets came the sounds of people who were coming and going, occupied with the business of daily life, people who are considered happy and worthy of envy by those who glimpse them from the heights of their own sorrows.

Now and then one would hear a verse or two from a fandango, with which some neighborhood servant girl alluded to her Sunday adventures, or with which the apprentice of a nearby shop killed time until the unfailing night arrived, and with it the agreed-upon meeting. . . . There sounded as well, in philosophical concert, the perpetual lullabies of the river's current, the confused noise of the capital, the rhythmic ticktock of the salon's pendulum clock, and the distant peal of bells that could have been tolling to announce a festival or a funeral, the baptism of a newborn baby or the taking of vows by another *comendadora* of the Order of Saint James.

All this, and the sun that would come back in search of our frigid climate, and that piece of blue firmament in which the eye and the soul would seek refuge, and those towers in the Alhambra, full of romantic and voluptuous memories, and the trees that flourished at their feet as they did when Granada was in Moorish hands . . . all this, all this must have weighed horribly on the soul of that thirty-year-old woman whose previous life had been the same as her present life and whose future existence could now be nothing more than a slow, continual repetition of such melancholy moments.

+++

The return of the little boy to the salon drew the nun out of her reverie and made the countess interrupt her reading again.

"Grandmother!" the youngster cried out in a harsh voice. "The Italian who's repairing the stone coat of arms on the staircase just said something very funny to the old man from Madrid who's painting the ceilings. I heard it without their seeing me, and since I understand now the broken Spanish that the sculptor speaks to the painter, I didn't lose a word! If you knew what he said!"

"Carlos," replied the elderly woman with the equivocal mildness of cowardice, "I have told you never to keep company with men of their sort. Remember that you are the Count of Santos!"

"Well, I want to be with them!" the child said. "I really like painters and sculptors and I'm going back to them again right now!"

"Carlos," the nun spoke sweetly, "you are talking to your father's mother. Respect her as he did and as I do."

The little boy started laughing and continued: "Well, Aunt, you'll see what the sculptor said. Because he was talking about you!"

"About me?"

"Hush, Carlos!" the elderly woman exclaimed severely.

The little boy continued in the same tone and with the same diabolical expression: "The sculptor said to the painter: 'My friend, how beautiful the nun must be naked! Like a Greek statue!' What's a Greek statue, Aunt Isabel?"

Sister Isabel turned livid, stared at the floor, and began to pray.

The countess got up, grabbed her grandson by the arm and said to him with repressed anger: "Children do not listen to such things, nor do they repeat them! The sculptor shall leave this house immediately. As for you, the chaplain will tell you what kind of sin you have committed and will give you the proper penance."

"*Me*? The priest give penance to *me*?" said Carlos. "I'm braver than he is and I'll throw him out into the street—and the sculptor stays!

"Aunt," the boy continued, "I want to see you naked."

"Good Lord!" his grandmother cried out, covering her face with her hands.

Sister Isabel did not even bat an eyelid.

"Yes, ma'am! I want to see my aunt naked!" repeated the little boy, facing the countess.

"You insolent child!" she shouted, raising her hand to her grandson.

Seeing her threatening gesture, the boy turned as red as a beet and, stamping his feet in a rage, as if ready to attack the countess, exclaimed in a flat tone: "I've said that I want to see my aunt naked! Slap me if you dare!"

The nun stood up with a disdainful air and headed toward the door, paying no attention at all to her nephew.

Carlos gave a start and blocked her way, repeating his terrible demand with the voice and symptom of true madness.

Sister Isabel continued walking away.

The little boy struggled to stop her, could not, and fell to the floor, seized by a violent convulsion.

His grandmother let out a bloodcurdling scream that caused the *comendadora* to turn her head.

And the latter stopped in her tracks, frightened, when she saw her nephew there on the floor, rolling his eyes, foaming at the mouth and stammering fiercely: "See . . . my aunt . . . naked!"

"Satan!" the nun blurted out, staring at her mother.

The child wriggled on the floor like a snake, turned purple, called out to his aunt again, and then lay motionless, stiff and out of breath.

"The Santos heir is dying!" the grandmother cried out with indescribable terror. "Water! Water! A doctor!"

The servants came on the run, bringing water and vinegar.

The countess sprinkled the boy's face with both, kissed him repeatedly, and called him "angel." She cried, she prayed, and she made him smell the vinegar. But it was all in vain. By fits and starts Carlos shook like someone possessed of the devil, opened his vacant, sightless eyes, which filled the onlookers with terror, and then lay motionless again.

The nun continued to stand still in the middle of the room, as though ready to leave, but with her head turned back, looking thoughtfully at her brother's son.

Finally the boy managed to let out a breath of air, and a few vague words slipped through his clamped, gnashing teeth.

Those words were. . . . "Naked . . . my aunt. . . ."

The nun raised her hands to heaven and continued on her way.

The grandmother, fearing that the servants might understand what the boy was saying, shouted imperiously: "Everybody out! But you stay, Isabel."

The servants obeyed, filled with amazement.

The *comendadora* fell to her knees.

"Carlos! My precious child! My beautiful child!" the countess wailed, embracing what already seemed like the corpse of her grandson. "Cry! Cry! Don't get angry! It'll be as you wish!"

"Naked!" said Carlos in a nasal voice similar to the death rattle.

"Isabel!" exclaimed the grandmother, looking at her daughter in a way that could not be defined. "The Santos heir is dying and with him our line dies out."

The nun shook from head to toe. As aristocratic as her mother and as pious and chaste as her mother, she understood all the enormity of the situation.

At this point Carlos recovered somewhat, saw both women, tried to get up, let out a furious yell, and suffered another attack even more terrible than the first one.

"See my aunt naked!" he roared before turning rigid again. And his fists clenched in a threatening gesture.

The elderly woman made the sign of the cross, picked up the prayer book, and started walking toward the door. Upon passing the *comendadora*, she raised her hand to heaven with painful solemnity and said: "Isabel . . . it is God's will!" And she left the salon, closing the door behind her.

IV

A half hour later, the Count of Santos entered his grandmother's room, hiccuping, laughing, eating a piece of candy—which had been wetted by tears during his seizure—and without looking at the elderly woman, but elbowing her, he said in a hoarse, flat voice: "Boy, is my aunt . . . fat!"

The countess, who was praying on her knees at an old prie-dieu, let her forehead fall on her prayer book and did not utter a word.

The child went off in search of the sculptor and found him surrounded by several agents of the Holy Office, who were showing him an order to follow them to the prisons of the Inquisition "for being a pagan and a blasphemer, according to the accusation made by the Countess of Santos."

Despite all his boldness, Carlos was seized with fear at the sight of the constables of the formidable Tribunal and neither said nor attempted to do a thing.

V

WHEN it grew dark, the countess went to her daughter's room before the lamps were lighted—because although she did not want to see her, she did wish to console her—and came across the following letter, which was handed to her by Sister Isabel's maid:

My dearest mother:

Forgive me for the first step that I am taking in my life without first seeking your permission, but my heart tells me that you will not disapprove.

I am returning to the convent which I never should have left, and which I shall never leave again. I am going without saying goodbye in order to spare you more suffering.

May God watch over you and be merciful to your loving
daughter,

Sister Isabel de los Ángeles

The elderly woman had not finished reading those heavy-
hearted lines when she heard a carriage roll out of the courtyard and then move off toward Plaza Nueva. It was the
carriage in which the *comendadora* was leaving.

VI

FOUR years later the bells of the Convent of the Order of
Saint James tolled for the soul of Sister Isabel de los Ángeles
as her body was given back to Mother Earth.

The countess also died shortly afterward.

Count Carlos departed this life without issue fifteen or
twenty years later, during the conquest of Menorca, and with
him died out the noble line of the Counts of Santos.

Captain Poison

Part I
BODILY WOUNDS

I

A Little Political History

ON the afternoon of 26 March 1848 there was gunfire and knife fighting in Madrid between a handful of civilians who shouted with their last breaths the until then foreign cry of "Long live the republic!" and the army of the Spanish monarchy (brought or created by Ataúlfo, reconstituted by Don Pelayo, and reorganized by Trastamara*), whose ostensible commander-in-chief was, in the name of Doña Isabel II, Don Ramón María Narváez,* President of the Council of Ministers and Minister of War.

And this is enough about history and politics, so let us move on to write about less well-known and more agreeable things, which were brought to pass or occasioned by those regrettable events.

II

Our Heroine

ON the left-hand side of the first floor of a humble but pleasant and clean apartment house on Calle de Preciados, a very narrow and crooked street back then and scene of the clash on that March afternoon, there lived alone, that is to say, without the company of a single man, three good, devout women who were very different from one another in physical makeup and social status. The first was an elderly widow from Guipúzcoa,* of solemn and distinguished mien; the second was her daughter, young, single, and quite attractive, although in a way different than her mother, which showed that she had taken after her father in everything; and the third was a servant, impossible to portray or describe, of indeterminate age, figure, and even sex, baptized, after a fashion, in Mondoñedo,* to whom we have already shown too much kindness, like the priest who administered the sacrament, by recognizing that she belonged to the human race.

The aforementioned young woman looked like the symbol or representation, alive and dressed in skirts, of common sense, such was the balance between her beauty and her naturalness, between her elegance and her simplicity, between her gracefulness and her modesty. It was as easy as pie for her to escape notice out on the street and not arouse the interest of the professional Don Juans, but impossible for anyone not to admire her and be captivated by her many charms after taking heed of her. She was not, or rather, did not want to be, one of those fulminating, ostentatious, showy beauties who attract all the looks as soon as they appear at a salon, theater, or promenade, and who compromise or completely overshadow the poor devils that escort them, be they fiancés, husbands, fathers, or fabulous potentates.* She was a harmonious and sensible blend of moral and physical perfections whose remarkable steadiness did not excite enthusiasm at first, as peace and order do not excite enthusiasm; put another way, she could be likened to well-proportioned monuments in which nothing surprises or amazes us until we make the judgment that, if everything turns out to be even, simple, and natural, it is because all parts are equally beautiful. It might be said that this honorable, middle-class goddess had studied her manner of dressing, combing, looking, moving, carrying, in short, the treasures of her splendid youth, in such a way that one would not consider her conceited, or smug, or provocative, but very different from the marriageable deities who show off their charms and go everywhere, saying to everybody: "This house is for sale . . . or for rent."

But let us not dwell on witticisms or descriptions, for we have much to relate and precious little time to do so.

III

Our Hero

THE republicans were firing at the soldiers from the corner of Calle de Peregrinos, and the soldiers were firing at the republicans from the Puerta del Sol,* so that the bullets of both sides were passing in front of the windows of the abovementioned first floor and would, from time to time, strike the iron bars of their grilles, causing them to vibrate stridently, ricocheting off blinds, wood frames, and panes.

The mother and the servant experienced the same profound terror, even though for each one it was different in nature and expression. The noble widow feared first for her daughter, then for the rest of the human race, and lastly for herself. The Galician servant, on the other hand, feared first and foremost for her own beloved skin, secondly, for her and her mistresses' stomachs, because the water jug was nearly empty and the baker had not delivered the afternoon bread, and thirdly, a little for the soldiers or her compatriots from Galicia who might die or lose a limb in the fight. And we make no mention of the daughter's terror because, whether her curiosity neutralized it or it did not penetrate her spirit, which was more manly than feminine, the fact was that—turning a deaf ear to her mother's advice and orders, as well as to the servant's wailing or moaning—while both hid on the inside, this genteel young woman would slip out to the rooms that faced the street, and would even open the wood shutters of a grille, to form an exact idea of the state and progress of the fight.

During one of these quick glimpses, which were extremely dangerous, she saw that the troops had already advanced to the door of the house, while the seditionists were retreating toward the Plaza de Santo Domingo and continuing to fire in echelon with admirable calm and bravery. And she also saw that at the head of the soldiers, and even of the officers and commanders, there stood out, for his energetic, intrepid attitude and for the fiery language with which he was haranguing them, a man of about forty, with a distinguished, well-bred air and refined and noble, although hard, features, a man who was thin and strong like a bundle of nerves, on the tall side, and dressed partly in mufti, partly in uniform. By this we mean that he wore a forage cap with the three stripes of a captain's insignia, but black civilian frock coat and pants, and carried the saber of an infantry officer in one hand and a cartridge belt and a shotgun, not an army issue, but one for hunting rabbits and partridges, in the other.

The young Madrilenian woman was watching and admiring this singular individual when the republicans fired a volley at him, no doubt because they considered him more fearsome than all the others, or assumed that he was a general, minister, or the like, and the poor captain, or whatever he was, fell to the ground as if struck by lightning, his face awash with blood, while the rebels were fleeing joyously, very satisfied with their deed, but with the soldiers hard on their heels and itching to avenge their unfortunate leader.

So the street ended up empty and silent, and in the middle of it lay that bleeding gentleman who perhaps had not yet died, and whom kind, solicitous hands might deliver from death. The young woman did not hesitate an instant; she ran to where her mother and the servant were and explained to them what had happened, adding that on Calle de Preciados there was no more firing. She had to battle against not so much the highly sensible objections of the generous Guipuzcoan native as against the purely animal fear of the shapeless Galician servant, but a few minutes later the three women carried to their modest home and put in the master bedroom, on the widow's luxurious bed, the unconscious body of the man who, if he was not the real protagonist of the expedition of 26 March, is going to be the leading character of our particular story.

IV

One's Own Skin and Another's

IT did not take long for the charitable women to realize that the gallant captain was not dead, merely unconscious and deprived of his senses as a result of a bullet wound that had grazed his forehead without penetrating it. They also realized that his right leg had been pierced and was possibly broken, and that not for an instant should they neglect that wound, from which flowed a great deal of blood. They realized, in a word, that the only really useful and efficacious thing they could do for the poor fellow was to summon a doctor immediately.

"Mama," said the brave young woman, "Dr. Sánchez lives just a few steps away, in the house across the street. Have Rosa go and bring him here. It would only take a moment and there would be no danger."

Just then a shot was heard nearby, followed by four or five others, fired simultaneously and further away. Afterwards a profound silence reigned again.

"I'm not going anywhere!" the servant grumbled. "What we heard just now were shots too, and my mistresses won't want me to get killed crossing the street."

"Silly! Nothing's happening in the street!" exclaimed the young woman, who had just looked out of one of the grilles.

"Get away from there, Angustias!" shrieked the mother,

seeing where her daughter was.

"The first shot that we heard," continued saying the now identified Angustias, "the one that was answered by the troops at the Puerta del Sol, must have been fired from the attic at number 19, by a very ugly man, because I can see him reloading his blunderbuss. The bullets, therefore, are passing overhead, and there's no danger at all in crossing the street. So I think it would be unforgivable if we were to let this poor devil die to save ourselves a little bit of trouble."

"I'll go after the doctor," said the mother as she finished bandaging the captain's broken leg.

"No, you won't!" exclaimed the daughter upon entering the bedroom. "What would people say about me? I'll go because I'm younger and I walk faster. You've suffered enough in this world on account of these cursed wars!"

"But nevertheless you're not going," the mother responded imperiously.

"I'm not either," added the servant.

"Mama, let me go! I ask you in the name of my father's memory! I don't have the stomach to watch this brave man bleed to death when we can save him. Look, look! Your bandages aren't doing him any good. Blood is already seeping through the mattress."

"Angustias, I've said you're not going!"

"I won't go if you don't want me to, but think, Mother: my poor father, your noble and valiant husband, would not have died as he did, would not have bled to death in the middle of a forest the night of an engagement, if some compassionate hand had stanched his wounds."

"Angustias!"

"Mama, let me go! I'm as Aragonese* as my father, even though I was born in this degenerate Madrid. Besides, I don't believe that we women have been granted a papal bull dispensing us from having as much self-respect and courage as men."

Thus did that spirited young woman speak, and her mother had not yet recovered from an astonishment accompanied by moral submission or involuntary applause, when Angustias was already intrepidly crossing Calle de Preciados.

V

A Blunderbuss Shot

"LOOK, Señora! Look what a beautiful figure she cuts!" exclaimed the servant, clapping her hands as she watched our heroine from the grille.

But, alas, at that very instant a shot rang out close by, and since the poor widow, who had also come to the window, saw her daughter stop and feel her clothes, she let out a heartrending scream and fell to her knees, nearly senseless.

"Hit she wasn't! Hit she wasn't!" shouted the servant meanwhile. "She's going into the house across the street now. Control yourself, Señora."

But the latter did not hear her. As pale as a corpse, she was struggling with her prostration, until, finding strength in the pain itself, she got up, beside herself, and ran out into the street . . . in the middle of which she met the undaunted Angustias, who was on her way back, followed by the doctor.

Mother and daughter embraced and kissed in a veritable frenzy, right over the pool of blood that had been spilled by the captain, and finally went inside the house without anyone realizing in those first few moments that the young woman's skirts were riddled by the treacherous blunderbuss shot fired at her by the man in the attic when he saw her crossing the street.

It was the Galician servant who not only noticed it but was cruel enough to call attention to it. "Hit she was! Hit she was!" she exclaimed in her Mondoñedo grammar. "I was right not to go out! Those bullets would have made nice holes in my three petticoats!"

Let us imagine for a moment the poor mother's renewed terror, until Angustias convinced her that she was unharmed. But the reader should understand that, as we shall see soon enough, the unfortunate woman from Guipúzcoa was not to enjoy another hour of good health from that day forward. And now let us turn our attention to the stricken captain to see what assessment is made of his wounds by the diligent and skilled Doctor Sánchez.

VI

Diagnosis and Prognosis

SAID doctor had an enviable reputation, and he justified it again with the swift and effective first aid that he administered to our hero, stopping the flow of blood from his wounds with household medicines and setting and splinting his fractured leg with only the three women for assistants. But as an exponent of his science, he did not acquit himself as well, for the good man suffered from the oratorical vice of speaking platitudes.*

Naturally, he said that the captain would not die, "provided that within twenty-four hours he came out of that profound daze," which indicated a grave concussion caused by the lesion that an oblique projectile, a projectile shot by a firearm, had produced in his forehead, without shattering, although certainly contusing, the frontal bone, "in the exact location of the wound, as a consequence of our unfortunate civil discord and that man having been caught up in it." And he promptly added, by way of clarification, that if the above-mentioned concussion did not run its course within the stated time period, the captain would most assuredly die, "which would be proof that the projectile's blow had been too strong. But, with respect to whether or not the concussion would run its course within twenty-four hours, he was reserving his prognosis until the following afternoon."

Having spoken these monumental truths, he strongly recommended, and to the point of being tiresome (no doubt because well did he know the daughters of Eve), that when the wounded captain regained consciousness they were not to allow him to talk, nor were they to talk to him about a thing, as urgent as it might seem to them to start a conversation with him. He left verbal instructions and written prescriptions to cover all the contingencies that might arise, and agreed to return the next day even if there were more gunfire, to show that he was as honorable a man as he was a good doctor and naive orator. But before he went back home, in case he was needed in another similarly pressing situation, he advised the agitated widow to go to bed early because she had an irregular pulse, and it was very possible that she would have a slight fever when night fell, and it had already fallen.

<h2 style="text-align:center">VII</h2>

Expectation

It was about three o'clock in the morning, and although the noble lady did indeed feel unwell, she continued at the bedside of her sick guest, ignoring the entreaties of the tireless Angustias, who was not only keeping watch also, but had not sat down all night long.

As erect and still as a statue, the young woman stood at the foot of the bloodstained bed with her eyes fixed on the sharp, white face, like a Christ carved in ivory, of that brave warrior whom she had admired so much in the afternoon, and in this way waited with evident anxiety for the poor devil to awaken from the profound lethargy that could possibly end in death.

Meanwhile, the fortunate servant was snoring to her heart's content in the drawing room, with her clear brow resting on her knees, unaware that her armchair had a back support for the head.

During that long vigil, mother and daughter had exchanged several observations and guesses about not only what the captain's social status might be but also his character, his ideas, and his sympathies. With the attention to detail that women never fail to pay, even in the most terrible and solemn circumstances, they had taken note of the fine quality of his shirt, of his expensive pocket watch, of his personal cleanliness, and of the little coronets of a marquis on his socks. Nor did they fail to notice a very old gold medal that their patient wore around his neck, under his clothes, nor that the medal represented the Virgin of the Pillar of Zaragoza,* all of which gladdened them exceedingly, concluding as they did that the captain was a person of standing, a person of a good and Christian upbringing. What they respected, naturally, was the inside of his pockets, where perhaps there were letters or cards with his name and address, information that they hoped to God he would be able to give them himself when he regained consciousness and his power of speech, as a sign that he still had a life to live.

Although the political fracas had ceased by then, with the forces of the monarchy victorious, the two women would hear from time to time, if not a distant, unanswered report like the solitary protest of some republican or other not subdued by shrapnel, then the loud hoofbeats of cavalry patrols making the rounds and assuring public order, both of which sounds were mournful and ominous, very dismal to hear from the bedside of a wounded and half-dead army officer.

VIII

Drawbacks of the Stranger's Guidebook*

THUS did things stand when, shortly after the clock of the Church of El Buen Suceso struck three-thirty, the captain all of a sudden opened his eyes and cast a sullen glance around the room. Staring with a kind of puerile terror, first at Angustias and then at her mother, he stammered irritably: "Where the devil am I?"

The young woman put a finger to her lips to indicate to him that he should keep silent, but the widow had taken exception to the third word of that question and quickly replied: "You are in an honorable and safe place, namely, in the home

of the widow of General Barbastro, Countess of Santurce, at
your service."

"Women! Hang it all!" stuttered the captain, half-closing his
eyes, as if he were slipping back into lethargy.

But very soon they noticed that he was breathing with the
ease and vigor of someone who is sleeping peacefully.

"He's pulled through!" Angustias exclaimed very softly. "My
father will be pleased with us."

"I was praying for his soul," her mother responded.
"Although you see that our patient's first greeting leaves a lot
to be desired."

"I know by heart," said the captain slowly, without opening
his eyes, "the roll of the General Staff of the Spanish Army,
inserted in the *Stranger's Guidebook*, and there does not
appear in it nor has there appeared in it in this century, any
General Barbastro."

"Let me tell you something!" the widow exclaimed sharply.
"My deceased husband—"

"Don't answer him now, Mama," interrupted her daughter,
smiling. "He's delirious and we have to be careful with his
poor head. Remember Dr. Sánchez's instructions."

"I am not delirious, Señorita. The thing is that I always
speak the truth to everybody, come what may."

And having said this, word for word, he sighed deeply, as
though very fatigued from so much talking, and began to
snore dully, like someone who was breathing his last.

"Are you asleep, Captain?" asked the widow, much
alarmed.

The wounded man did not answer.

IX

More Drawbacks of the *Stranger's Guidebook*

"LET'S let him rest," said Angustias softly, sitting down next
to her mother. "And since he can't hear us now, permit me,
Mama, to call your attention to something. I think it was

unwise of you to tell him you're a countess and a general's widow."

"Why?"

"Because . . . you know full well that we don't have sufficient means to look after and care for a person like this man in the way that real countesses and widows of generals would do."

"What do you mean 'real'?" the lady from Guipúzcoa asked sharply. "Are you also going to cast doubt on my status? I'm as much a countess as the Countess of Montijo* and as much a general's wife as the wife of General Espartero."*

"You're right, but until the government grants your petition for a widow's pension, we'll continue to be as poor as a church mouse."

"Not all that poor. I still have a thousand *reales* left from the emerald earrings, and I have a pearl necklace with diamond brooches, a present from my grandfather, that is worth more than five hundred *duros*. Together they give us more than enough to live on until my widow's pension is approved, which will be inside of a month, and also to care properly for this man, even if his broken leg obliges him to stay here for two or three months. You already know that the official on the review board believes that I qualify for benefits under article 10 of the Convention of Vergara,* because although your father died beforehand, it's clear that he had already reached an understanding with Maroto."*

"Santurce . . . Santurce. . . . That countship doesn't appear in the *Stranger's Guidebook* either," mumbled the captain without opening his eyes.

And then, all of a sudden shaking off his lethargy and managing to sit up in bed, he said in a strong, resonant voice, as if he were already well: "Let's speak plainly, Señora. I need to know where I am and who you ladies are. Nobody leads me around by the nose or pulls the wool over my eyes. The devil! How this leg hurts!"

"Captain, you are insulting us!" the general's widow snapped.

"Come now, Captain. Be still and no talking," Angustias said at the same time, softly, although firmly. "Your life will be in great danger if you don't keep silent or if you don't stay still. Your right leg is broken and a wound in your forehead rendered you unconscious for more than ten hours."

"You're right!" exclaimed that strange individual, raising his hands to his head and feeling the bandages the doctor had put on him. "Those scoundrels wounded me! But who's the imprudent soul that brought me to someone else's house when I have my own and there are civilian and military hospitals? I don't like to inconvenience anybody or owe favors, which I'm damned if I deserve or want to deserve! I was on Calle de Preciados—"

"And you still are on Calle de Preciados, No. 14, first floor," interrupted the Guipuzcoan, disregarding her daughter's sign language that she should keep quiet. "We don't need you to thank us for a thing, as we have done no more than what God commands and charity dictates. As to the rest, you are in a respectable home. I am Doña Teresa Carrillo de Albornoz y Azpeitia, widow of the Carlist General Don Luis Gonzaga de Barbastro, whose rank was acknowledged at Vergara. Do you understand? *Acknowledged at Vergara*, even if it was in a 'tacit, retrospective, and implicit' manner, as it says in my petitions. He owed his title of Count of Santurce to a royal appointment made by Carlos V,* which Doña Isabel II has to confirm in accordance with article 10 of the Convention of Vergara. I never lie, nor do I use assumed names, nor do I propose, in your case, anything other than caring for you and saving your life, now that Providence has entrusted me with this responsibility."

"Mama, don't encourage him," continued Angustias. "You can see that instead of accepting your explanation he's getting ready to answer you more forcefully. And the poor man's ill and weak in the head. Come now, Captain, calm down and don't endanger your life."

Thus spoke that noble young woman with her customary seriousness. But not on that account did the captain calm down; on the contrary, he stared at her with even greater fury, like a wild boar at bay that is attacked by a new and more formidable adversary, and exclaimed:

X

The Captain Explains Himself

"Señorita, in the first place I am not weak in the head, nor have I ever been, proof of which is that a bullet wasn't able to penetrate it. In the second place, I'm very sorry that you speak to me with so much commiseration and sympathy, since I don't understand gentleness, flattery, or prudery. Excuse the roughness of my language, but we are all as God created us, and I don't like to deceive anybody. I don't know by what law of nature I am as I am, but I'd rather be shot than treated kindly. Consequently, I advise both of you not to pamper me so much because you'll make me kick the bucket in this bed where my bad fortune has me tied down. I wasn't born to receive favors nor to be grateful for them nor to repay them, which is why I've always tried not to have dealings with women, children, sanctimonious sorts, or any other kind of peaceful, mild-mannered people. I'm an atrocious man whom no one can stand—not as a boy or a youth or the old man that I'm beginning to be. All over Madrid I'm called *Captain Poison*! So the two of you can go to bed and arrange first thing tomorrow morning to have me taken to the General Hospital on a stretcher. That's final."

"Good Lord, what a man!" exclaimed a horrified Doña Teresa.

"Everybody should be this way!" retorted the captain. "The world would be better off or it would have come to an end a long time ago!"

Angustias smiled again.

"Don't smile, Señorita, because that's making fun of a poor incapacitated man who's unable to run away in order to deliver you from his presence!" the captain continued, speaking with a hint of melancholy. "I know all too well that I must seem very ill-mannered to you both, but rest assured that I'm not too sorry about it. I would be sorry, on the other hand, if you considered me worthy of esteem and then later on accused me of having misled you. Oh, if I caught the rascal who brought me to this house just to annoy you and dishonor me—"

"I, the señora, and the señorita, we brought you here," said the Galician, who had been awakened and drawn to the bed by that madman's shouting. "The gentleman was bleeding to death at the door of this house when the señorita took pity on him. I also took some pity on him. And since the señora took pity on him too, the three of us carried the gentleman in our arms, and does he ever weigh in spite of how thin he looks!"

The captain had gotten into a huff again when another woman turned up, but the servant's account impressed him so much that he could not help exclaiming: "It's a shame that you didn't do this good deed for a better man than I am. Why did you need to make the acquaintance of the incorrigible Captain Poison?"

Doña Teresa glanced at her daughter as if to have her understand that their patient was not nearly as bad and ferocious a man as he believed, and she saw that Angustias still had a winsome smile on her face as a sign that she held the same opinion.

Meanwhile, the mournful Galician was saying tearfully: "Well, the gentleman would be even more ashamed if he knew that the señorita went in person to summon the doctor to treat those two bullet wounds, and that, when she was in the middle of the street, at her someone fired a shot that . . . look, made holes in her skirt!"

"I never would've told you about it, Captain, for fear of irritating you," the young woman explained half modestly and half mockingly, lowering her eyes and smiling even more winsomely than before. "But since Rosa here spills everything, I can't help begging you to forgive me for the scare that I threw into my dear mother, a scare that triggered her present feverish state."

The captain was astonished, gaping alternately at Angustias, at Doña Teresa, and at the servant, and when the young woman stopped talking, he closed his eyes, emitted a kind of bellow, and exclaimed, raising his fists to heaven: "Oh, you cruel women! How I feel the dagger in my wound! So the three of you have set out to make me your slave or laughing-stock? So you're bent on making me cry or say tender words? So I'm lost if I don't manage to escape? Well, then I'll escape! This is all I needed, that at my age I should become the plaything of the tyranny of three good women! You, Señora!" he continued emphatically, speaking to the widow. "If you do not go to bed right now, and do not drink, once under the covers, a cup of linden tea with orange blossom, I will tear off all these bandages and rags and die in five minutes, even though God may not will it. As for you, Señorita Angustias, kindly call the night watchman and tell him to go to the house of the Marquis of Los Tomillares, number —— on Carrera de San Francisco, to notify him that his cousin Don Jorge de Córdoba is waiting for him in this house, seriously wounded. Then you will also go to bed, leaving me in the clutches of this insufferable Galician woman, who from time to time will give me sugar water, the only assistance I shall require until my cousin Álvaro comes. So as I've said, Countess, you begin by going to bed."

Mother and daughter winked at each other, and the former replied agreeably: "I'm going to set you an example of obedience and reason. Goodnight, Captain. Until tomorrow."

"I too wish to be obedient," Angustias added, after taking down Captain Poison's real name and the address of his cousin's house. "But since I'm very sleepy, kindly permit me to wait until tomorrow before I have that thoughtful message sent to the Marquis of Los Tomillares. Goodnight, Don Jorge. Be careful not to move."

"I'm not staying alone with this gentleman!" the servant cried out. "His diabolical temper makes my hair stand on end and frightens the living daylights out of me!"

"Don't worry, beautiful," said the captain. "I'll be sweeter and nicer to you than to your young mistress."

Doña Teresa and Angustias could not help bursting into laughter upon hearing this first good-humored sally from their unbearable guest.

So it was that scenes as inauspicious and tragic as those of that afternoon and evening came to have, as a finishing, crowning touch, a little joy and gaiety. That's how certain it is that everything in this world is fleeting and transitory, happiness as well as sorrow, or, to put it another way, that's how certain it is that in this world nothing lasts forever.

Part II

THE BAD MAN'S LIFE

I

The Second Treatment

AT eight o'clock the following morning, which, through God's mercy, no longer showed signs of barricades or disturbances (mercy which was to last until 7 May* of that same year, when there occurred the terrible scenes of the Plaza Mayor), Dr. Sánchez was back in the home of the so-called Countess of Santurce, applying the final dressing to Captain Poison's broken leg.

The latter had taken it in his head to remain silent that morning. He had only opened his mouth up till then, before the beginning of the painful dressing operation, to direct two brief and gruff appeals to Doña Teresa and Angustias in response to their cordial "Good mornings."

He said to Doña Teresa: "For heaven's sake, Señora! Why did you get up if you're not well? Did you want to make my mortification and shame greater? Did you plan to kill me with kindness?"

And he said to Angustias: "What does it matter whether I'm better or worse? Let's come to the point. Have you sent for my cousin so that he can get me out of here? So that we can all be free of impertinences and ceremonies?"

"Yes, Captain Poison. The doorman's wife took the message to him a half hour ago," the young woman answered calmly, arranging the pillows for him.

As for the inflammable countess, needless to say she had again become piqued at her guest upon hearing still more of his incivility. She resolved, therefore, not to say another word to him and confined herself to making lint and bandages and asking Dr. Sánchez over and over again, with keen interest, how he found "the wounded captain" (without condescending to name him), and if he would end up lame, and if he could have chicken and ham broth at twelve, and if it would be desirable to cover the street with sand so that the noise of carriages would not bother him.

The physician, with his customary candor, assured her that there was no longer anything to fear from the bullet wound in his forehead, thanks to the vigorous and healthy constitution of the patient, in whom no symptoms of a concussion or fever remained, but his diagnosis was not as favorable with regard to the broken leg. He described it as grave and critical once again because the tibia was badly shattered, and he recommended to Don Jorge absolute immobility if he wished to save himself from an amputation and even from death itself.

The doctor spoke in such clear, plain language, not only for want of a knack for disguising his opinions, but because he had already formed a judgment of the headstrong and intractable character of that specimen of a spoiled child. But in truth he failed to frighten him; on the contrary, he wormed a smile of disbelief and mockery out of him.

The frightened ones were the three good women: Doña Teresa, out of sheer humanity; Angustias, out of a certain noble determination and pride that she now had in healing and domesticating such a heroic and strange individual; and the servant, out of an instinctive terror of everything that was blood, mutilation, and death.

The captain noticed the uneasiness of his nurses and, emerging from the calm with which he was enduring the treatment, said furiously to Dr. Sánchez: "Good Lord, man! You could've informed me of all these opinions when we were alone! Being a good doctor doesn't excuse you from being tactful. Look at these long, sad faces on my three Marys,* and it's all your fault."

At this point the patient had to stop talking, overcome by the terrible pain that the doctor caused him when he set the broken bone.

"Bah!" he continued presently. "And you think I'm going to stay in this house? Because I assure you that nothing infuriates me so much as seeing women cry!"

The poor captain stopped talking again and bit his lip for a few moments, although without uttering even a sigh. But there was no question that he was in considerable pain.

"As to the rest, Señora," he concluded, speaking to Doña Teresa, "I don't think there is any reason for you to be shooting those looks of hatred at me, because my cousin Álvaro can't be long in coming now, and he'll deliver you from Captain Poison! Then this doctor will see—goodness, man, don't press so hard!—how nicely, while ignoring that business of the 'absolute immobility'—hang it all, what a heavy touch you have!—four soldiers will carry me to my house on a stretcher, bringing all these scenes of a nuns' convent to an end. That's all I needed! Broth for *me*? Chicken broth for *me*? Put sand in the street for *me*? Am I by some chance a milksop of a soldier to be coddled so ridiculously?"

Doña Teresa was going to respond, resorting to the bellicose impulse that was her only weakness (without realizing, of course, that poor Don Jorge was suffering horribly), when, fortunately, someone knocked on the door and Rosa announced the Marquis of Los Tomillares.

"Thank God!" they all exclaimed at the same time, although in different tones and with different meanings.

And it was because the marquis's arrival had coincided with the conclusion of the treatment.

Don Jorge was perspiring from pain.

Angustias gave him a little water and vinegar, and the wounded man breathed contentedly, saying: "Thanks, beautiful."

At this juncture the marquis, led by Doña Teresa, came into the bedroom.

II

Rainbow of Peace

DON Álvaro de Córdoba y Álvarez de Toledo was a highly distinguished man about sixty years old, clean-shaven, and already shaved at that hour; he had a round, peaceful, kindly face that allowed the serenity and gentleness of his spirit to shine through; and so neat, stylish, and elegant was he in his dress that he looked like the statue of method and order.

And although it was clear that he was very moved and overcome by his relative's misfortune, he did not lose his composure, nor did he fail to observe the most scrupulous politeness. With the utmost courtesy he greeted Angustias, the doctor, and even acknowledged the Galician, although she had not been introduced to him by Señora Barbastro, and then, and only then, did he cast a long look at the captain, the look of an affectionate but austere father, as though consoling him and reprimanding him at the same time, and accepting, if not the cause, the consequences of that new escapade.

Meanwhile, Doña Teresa, and most of all the loquacious Rosa, who several times took care to mention her mistress by the two titles in legal dispute, *velis nolis** informed the ceremonious marquis of all that had happened in the house and the area around it since the previous afternoon when the first shot was heard, until that very instant, without omitting Don Jorge's aversion to allowing himself to be cared for and pitied by the three persons who had saved his life.

After the widow and servant stopped talking, the marquis questioned Dr. Sánchez, who informed him of the captain's wounds, the gist of which we already know, insisting that he must not be moved elsewhere, at the risk of compromising his recovery and even his life.

Finally, the good Don Álvaro turned to Angustias with a questioning gesture as if to see whether she wished to add anything to the account given by the others, and, seeing that the young woman just shook her head, His Excellency blew his nose, cleared his throat, and then, promptly assuming the grave attitude of a speaker before a senate, and he was a senator, said, half seriously, half good-naturedly: (But this speech should constitute a separate chapter, in case there is a desire to include it in the *Complete Works* of the marquis, who was also a man of letters, one of those who are called "to the manner born.")

III

The Power of Eloquence

"LADIES and gentlemen: in the midst of the tribulation that afflicts us, and overlooking political considerations with regard to yesterday's woeful events, it seems to me that we cannot complain at all—"

"You should talk. 'Cannot complain.' Nothing's hurting you! But when does my turn to talk come?" interrupted Captain Poison.

"Yours will not come, my dear Jorge," the marquis replied smoothly. "I know you too well to have any need for you to explain to me your positive or negative acts. I am content with the account given me by these good people."

The captain, in whom we have already noticed the profound respect, or scorn, with which he systematically refrained from contradicting his illustrious cousin, crossed his arms philosophically, fixed his eyes on the bedroom ceiling, and began to whistle the Riego Hymn.*

"I was saying," continued the marquis, "that from the worst of circumstances has come the best. My incorrigible and beloved relative Don Jorge de Córdoba brought this new misfortune on himself, because nobody ordered him to meddle in yesterday afternoon's scrap; he is in the reserves, according to custom, and could have saved himself the trouble of imitating books of chivalry.* But it is a misfortune that has a most agreeable remedy, or has had one, and happily at the opportune moment, thanks to the heroism of this gallant young lady, to the charitable assistance of Señora Barbastro, Countess of Santurce, to the skill of the worthy doctor of medicine and surgery, Señor Sánchez, whose reputation I have known for many years, and to the zeal of this tireless servant."

Here the Galician began to cry.

"Let us go on to the dispositive part," continued the marquis, in whom, apparently, the organ of classification and demarcation predominated and who, consequently, could have been a great agronomist. "Ladies and gentlemen: inasmuch as in the opinion of medical science, as well as common sense, it would be dangerous in the extreme to move our interesting patient and my first cousin, Don Jorge de Córdoba, from this hospitable bed, I resign myself to his continuing to disturb this peaceful dwelling until such time that he can be taken to my house or to his. But let it be understood that all this is based on the assumption, dear relative, that your generous heart and the illustrious name that you bear will induce you to dispense with certain bad habits picked up at school, the barracks, and the casino, and save from discontent and unpleasantness this respectable lady and her worthy daughter who, ably seconded by their active and robust maid, rescued you from death in the middle of the street. Don't answer back, cousin! You know that I think things over carefully before making up my mind, and that I never rescind my orders. As to the rest, the señora and I shall speak alone—whenever it is convenient for her, because I'm never in a rush—about insignificant details of procedure that will give a natural and admissible character to what will always be, at bottom, a great act of charity on her part. And since I have now clarified, through this brief speech, for which I did not come prepared, all aspects and phases of the matter, I yield the floor for the present. I have spoken."

The captain continued whistling the Riego Hymn, and we believe even those of Bilbao and Maella, with his irate eyes still so fixed on the bedroom ceiling that it is a wonder it did not start to burn or fall to the floor.

Angustias and her mother, upon seeing their enemy

vanquished, had tried two or three times to catch his attention, so as to calm him down or console him with their gentle and benevolent attitude, but he had answered them with rapid and bitter gestures which were very similar to oaths of revenge, returning at once to his patriotic music with a more spirited and ardent expression.

One might say that he was a lunatic in the presence of his keeper, for it was no other role that the marquis played in that scene.

IV

Indispensable Preambles

As an experienced physiologist and psychologist who had understood and assessed everything, as if it were a situation that involved automatons and not people, Dr. Sánchez withdrew at this point, and then the marquis again asked the widow to grant him a few minutes' private audience.

Doña Teresa led him to her boudoir, located at the opposite end of the drawing room, and once the two sexagenarians were both settled in armchairs, the man of the world began by asking for a glass of warmed sugar water, claiming that it fatigued him to speak twice in succession ever since he delivered a speech in the Senate against railroads and telegraphs that took three days. But what he actually had in mind when asking for water was to give the lady from Guipúzcoa time to explain to him the generalship and the countship that the good man had not heard about before, and which were of great moment, given that they were going to discuss money.

The reader can imagine with how much pleasure the poor woman must have unbosomed herself about such a matter as soon as Don Álvaro brought it up. She related her petition from A to Z, without forgetting the question of the "tacit, retrospective, and implicit" right to have enough to live on, a right guaranteed to her under article 10 of the Convention of

Vergara; and when she had nothing more to say and began to fan herself as a sign of truce, the Marquis of Los Tomillares took the floor and spoke as follows:

(But it would be better if his interesting account also formed a separate chapter, as it is a model of expository analysis that could figure in Volume XX of his *Works* with the title *About My Relatives, Friends, and Servants*.)

V

The Captain's History

"YOU have the misfortune, Countess, to lodge in your home one of the most complex and uncivil men that God has brought into the world. I won't say that he strikes me as a demon through and through, but one does need the patience of a saint, or to love him as I love him by the law of nature and pity, in order to put up with his impertinence, ferocity, and madness. Suffice it to say that the dissolute and fearless crowd with which he associates at the casino and in the cafés gave him the nickname Captain Poison on seeing that he's always hopping mad and ready to come to blows with everyone and anyone over some trifle. Let me hasten to add, though, for your peace of mind and that of your family, that he is chaste and a man of honor and integrity, not only incapable of offending any lady's modesty but excessively shy and reserved with the fair sex. I'll say more: perpetual irascibility and all, he has yet to do any real harm to anyone, unless it be to himself. And when it comes to yours truly, you've no doubt seen that he treats me with the deference due to a kind of older brother or surrogate father. But even so, I repeat that it's impossible to live with him, as is demonstrated most eloquently by the fact that, although he is a bachelor and I a widower and we have no other relatives, attachments, or presumptive and potential heirs, he doesn't live in my too spacious house, as the stubborn fool would if he wanted to, because by nature and upbringing, I'm very long-suffering, tolerant, and accommodating with people who respect my tastes, habits, ideas, hours, residences, and pastimes. It's this mild manner of mine that obviously makes us incompatible in private life, as several attempts have already shown, since he is exasperated by gentle and courteous ways, tender and affectionate scenes, and everything that isn't rough, harsh, strong, and aggressive. Naturally! He grew up without a mother and even without a nursemaid. His mother died giving birth to him, and his father, not wanting to fight with wetnurses, found him a goat, a wild one apparently, whose milk took their place. He was educated in private schools, as a boarder, from the very moment that he was weaned, because his father, my poor brother Rodrigo,* committed suicide shortly after becoming a widower. As a beardless youth, he fought in the war in America, among savages, and from there he returned to take sides in our civil discord of seven years.* He would be a general now if he hadn't quarreled with every one of his superiors from the time he first began to wear the aiguillettes of a cadet. And the few promotions and postings that he has gotten up to now have cost him wonders of bravery and countless wounds, without which he would not have been recommended for advancement by his commanding officers, always at odds with him on account of the bitter truths that he's in the habit of telling them. He's been under arrest sixteen times, and four times in various castles—in each instance for insubordination. What he's never done is rise in revolt! Since the end of the war, he's been in the reserves, continuously, because, although I've managed in my days of political favor to have him given this or that assignment in military offices or regiments, within twenty-four hours he's been sent home. Two ministers of war have been challenged to a duel by him, and he hasn't been shot yet out of respect for my name and his indisputable bravery. Despite all these mistakes, and in view of the fact that he had lost his slender fortune playing *tute** at that disreputable Prince's Casino and that his reservist's pay wasn't enough for him to live as befitted his social standing, I had the peculiar notion seven years ago of appointing him steward of my household and estate, which

had been swiftly disentailed on account of the successive
deaths of the last three owners—my father and my brothers
Alfonso and Enrique—and considerably neglected and
rundown as a result of these frequent changes of masters.
Without doubt, Providence inspired me with such a daring
thought! From that day forward, my affairs became orderly
and prosperous. Old and disloyal administrators lost their
positions or were transformed into saints, and by the following year my income had doubled—at present it has very
nearly quadrupled—because of the growth that Jorge has
spurred in livestock. I can say that today I have the best
sheep in Lower Aragón, all of them at your disposal! To
accomplish such marvels, all that madcap needed to do was
make one visit, on horseback, to all my properties, carrying
his saber in his hand like a baton, and work one hour a day
at the offices in my home. He earns a salary of 30,000 *reales*,
and I don't give him more because all that he has left, after
seeing to his meals and clothes—his only needs, and they're
moderate and reasonable—he loses at *tute* the last day of
every month. Let's not even talk about his reservist's pay,
inasmuch as it's always subject to the costs of a disciplinary
action stemming from insubordination. In a word: despite
everything, I love him and feel sorry for him like a headstrong son, and not having had any of my own, good or bad,
in my three marriages, and since my noble title shall pass to
him by statutory law, I intend to leave him my sound fortune
in its entirety, something the big fool hasn't guessed, and
Heaven forbid that he should, because if he did know he
would resign his position as steward or try to ruin me so that
I would never consider him personally interested in the
appreciation of my assets. The poor devil undoubtedly
believes, judging by appearances and slanderous gossip,
that I intend to name as my heir a certain niece of my last
wife, and I do not disabuse him for the reasons I have just
given. Imagine, then, what a bolt from the blue it will be for
him on the day that he inherits my millions, all nine of them,
and what a splash he'll make in the world with so much
money! I am certain that within three months he'll either be
president of the Council of Ministers and Minister of War or

that General Narváez will have executed him. My greatest pleasure would have been to marry him off, to see if matrimony tamed and domesticated him, and if I would be beholden to him, at a remove, for my long-held hopes of a successor to my title of marquis. But Jorge cannot fall in love, and would not admit it even if he did, and no woman would be able to live with a hothead like him. Such is, impartially drawn, our famous Captain Poison, on which account I beg you to have the patience to put up with him for a few weeks, in the assurance that I shall know how to express my gratitude for everything that you may do for his health and his life, as if you were to do it for me."

The marquis took out and unfolded his handkerchief upon concluding this part of his discourse and wiped his forehead with it, even though he was not perspiring. Then he refolded it at once, put it in the left back pocket of his frock coat, pretended to take a sip of water, and resumed speaking, changing both his attitude and his tone:

VI

The Rebel Leader's Widow

"LET us now speak of trifling matters, unbecoming, to a certain extent, to people of our standing, but ones with which we must necessarily deal. Fate, Countess, has brought to this house, and prevents him from leaving it in forty or fifty days, a perfect stranger to you, Don Jorge de Córdoba, about whom you had never heard a thing, and who has a millionaire relative. Now, as you have just told me, you are not rich—"

"I am so!" the lady from Guipúzcoa bravely interrupted.

"No, you're not, a point that does you great honor inasmuch as your magnanimous husband went broke in defense of the most noble cause. I, Señora, am also somewhat of a Carlist."

"It wouldn't matter if you were Don Carlos in the flesh!

Speak to me of another subject, sir, or let us consider this conversation ended! That's all I would need, to accept another's money in order to fulfill my duties as a Christian!"

"But, Señora, you are not a doctor, nor a druggist, nor—"

"My purse will be all of that for your cousin. The many times that my husband was wounded in defense of Don Carlos—except the last time, when, undoubtedly as punishment for being in league with that traitor Maroto, no one came to his aid and he bled to death in the middle of a forest—he was helped by peasants from Navarra and Aragón who accepted neither reimbursement nor gifts of any kind. I shall do the same for Don Jorge de Córdoba, whether or not his millionaire family agrees!"

"Nevertheless, Countess, I cannot accept such a thing," declared the marquis, half pleased and half annoyed.

"What you can never do is deprive me of the high honor that Heaven afforded me yesterday. My deceased husband told me that when a merchant ship or a man-of-war comes across a castaway in the solitude of the sea and saves him from death, he is received on board with royal honors, even though he may be a humble sailor. The crew climbs up on the yards, a rich carpet is spread on the starboard accommodation ladder, and the band and drums play the Royal March of Spain. Do you know why? Because in that castaway the crew sees someone sent by Providence! So I'm going to do the same thing for your cousin. I shall place at his feet all of my poverty by way of a carpet, as I would place all of my millions if I had them."

"Countess!" exclaimed the marquis, weeping openly. "Permit me to kiss your hand."

"And permit me, dearest Mama, to embrace you full of pride!" added Angustias, who had overheard the whole conversation from the doorway of the drawing room.

Doña Teresa also started to cry at seeing herself so applauded and praised. And as the servant, noticing that the others were in tears, did not waste an opportunity to cry either, she knew not why, there arose in the boudoir such a confusion of sobs, sighs, and expressions of goodwill that I'm better off changing the subject lest my readers also begin to cry uncontrollably and I end up without a public to whom to continue telling my poor story.

VII

Angustias's Suitors

"JORGE," said the marquis to Captain Poison, entering the bedroom with the air of someone about to bid farewell, "I'm leaving you here. The countess has refused to let us even foot the bills of the doctor and the druggist, so you'll be cared for here as you would be in your own mother's home, if she were alive. I need not remind you of the obligation that you're under to treat these ladies pleasantly and civilly, in keeping with your good upbringing, about which I have no doubts, and with the examples of courtesy and politeness that I have given you, because it is the very least that you can and should do in honor of such illustrious and charitable people. With the gracious countess's permission, I'll come back in the afternoon and have linen brought to you, as well as cigarettes and the things most urgently in need of your signature. Tell me if you want anything else from your house or mine."

"You don't say!" replied the captain. "Well, since you're being so considerate, why don't you bring me a little cotton wool and smoked glasses?"

"What for?"

"The cotton wool to stop up my ears and not hear idle words, and the smoked glasses so that no one can read in my eyes the atrocities that I'm thinking about."

"The devil you say!" replied the marquis, unable to maintain his grave demeanor, as Doña Teresa and Angustias could not suppress their laughter.

And at this point the magnate said goodbye to the two women, using the most affectionate and warm of expressions, as though he had known and socialized with them for a long time.

"An excellent person!" exclaimed the widow, looking at the captain out of the corner of her eye.

"A very kind gentleman!" said the servant, clutching a gold coin that the marquis had given her.

"A meddler!" grumbled the wounded man, facing the silent Angustias. "He's what you women would like all men to be! Oh, traitor! Angel! Flatterer! Magpie! Nuns' cohort! I won't die without paying him back for the dirty trick he's played on me today by leaving me in the hands of my enemies. As soon as I get well I'll say goodbye to him and his office and apply for a post as prison commandant, so I can live among people who won't irritate me with displays of honesty and sensitivity. Listen here, Señorita Angustias, will you tell me why you're laughing at me? Is there something funny about me?"

"Funny? I'm laughing because I'm thinking of how ugly you'll look with smoked glasses."

"So much the better! That way you'll escape the danger of falling in love with me!" the captain replied furiously.

Angustias burst out laughing; Doña Teresa turned green; and the Galician started to talk like a blue streak: "My señorita is not in the habit of falling in love with anybody! Since I've been here she's given the air to a druggist from Calle Mayor, who has a carriage; to the lawyer handling the señora's lawsuit, who's a millionaire, although somewhat older than you; and to three or four suitors in Retiro Park."*

"Be quiet, Rosa!" said the mother wistfully. "Don't you realize that these are . . . bouquets that the gallant captain is throwing at us? Fortunately his cousin has explained to me everything that I needed to know with respect to the character of our gracious guest. So I'm glad to see him in such good humor. If only this bothersome fatigue of mine would permit me to crack jokes too!"

The captain had turned rather sullen, as if devising some excuse or apology to make to mother and daughter. But it only occurred to him to say, with the voice and expression of a sulky little boy who is listening to reason: "Angustias, when this confounded leg doesn't hurt so much, we'll play *tute.* What do you say?"

"It will be a signal honor for me," the young lady answered, giving him the medicine he was scheduled to take then, "but let me warn you at the outset, Captain Poison, that I intend to take you to the cleaners!"

Don Jorge gave her a wide-eyed look and smiled sweetly for the first time in his life.

Part III

SPIRITUAL WOUNDS

I

Skirmishes

Amid conversations and squabbles of this nature, fifteen or twenty days went by and the captain's recovery progressed considerably. Only a slight scar remained on his forehead, and the bone of his leg was gradually knitting.

"This man has the constitution of an ox!" the doctor was wont to say.

"Thanks for the compliment, you diabolical quack!" the captain would respond with affectionate familiarity. "When I'm up and around I'm going to take you to bullfights and cockfights because you're every inch a man, a man with the guts to mend broken bodies."

Doña Teresa and her guest had also taken a real liking to each other, even though they were always bickering. Day in and day out Don Jorge would contend that she could not be granted a widow's pension, which would infuriate the lady from Guipúzcoa; but almost in the same breath he would invite her to sit down in the bedroom and tell her that, although not by the title of "General" or "Count," he had heard references any number of times during the civil war to the "rebel leader Barbastro" as one of the bravest and most distinguished, as well as most humane and chivalrous, Carlist commanders. But when he saw her sad and taciturn

81

as a result of her worries and ailments, he refrained from poking fun at the claim and called her, in a perfectly natural way, "Countess" and "general's wife," a mark of regard that would revitalize her and gladden her on the spot, and if not this, as a native of Aragón, and to remind the poor widow of her love for the deceased Carlist, he would hum *jotas* from that land that ended up making her laugh and cry at the same time.

These kindnesses on Captain Poison's part and, most of all, the singing of the Aragonese *jotas*, were the exclusive privilege of the mother, because as soon as Angustias approached the bedroom, they came to a complete halt and the patient would assume a fierce look. One would think that he loathed the pretty woman, perhaps on account of the very fact that he never succeeded in arguing with her, nor in seeing her cross, nor in getting her to take seriously the silly things that he said to her, nor in drawing her out of that somewhat sardonic seriousness that the poor devil characterized as a "constant insult."

It was worth noting, however, that on the days that Angustias came in late to say good morning to him, Don Jorge acted the saucy rogue and would ask over and over again in his dreadful-man fashion: "So where is she? Miss Queasiness. The shirker. Has her ladyship not yet awakened? Why has she permitted you to rise so early but not brought me my chocolate? Tell me, Doña Teresa, is the young Princess of Santurce by some chance ill?"

All the above was if he addressed the mother, but if he spoke to the Galician he would say with greater fury: "Listen here and mark my words, you monster from Mondoñedo! Tell your insufferable mistress that it's eight o'clock and I'm hungry, and that there's no reason for her to come so well-combed and pleasing to the eye, as usual. Because in any event, if she doesn't show up soon there won't be any *tute* today."

The *tute* was a farce, and even a daily drama. The captain played better than Angustias, but Angustias was luckier, and so the cards ended up flying toward the ceiling or toward the drawing room from the hands of that forty-year-old little boy who could not stand the supremely gracious calm with which the young woman would say to him: "Do you see, Captain Poison, how I'm the only person ever born to take you to the cleaners?"

II

The Issue Is Raised

MATTERS stood at this point when one morning the decision to open or not open the bedroom window, since it was a magnificent spring day, triggered a serious exchange between Don Jorge and his lovely adversary that went as follows:

CAPTAIN: It drives me crazy that you never contradict me or get annoyed at hearing me talk nonsense. You despise me! If you were a man, I swear that we would have it out with daggers.

ANGUSTIAS: Well, if I were a man I would laugh at all of that foul temper, the same as I laugh at it being a woman. And nevertheless we would be very good friends.

CAPTAIN: Friends? You and I? Impossible! You have the infernal ability to dominate and exasperate me with your prudence. I would never become your *friend* but your *slave*. And so as not to be one, I would propose that we fight to the death. All of this . . . if you were a man, but being a woman as you are—"

ANGUSTIAS: Continue. Don't be unstinting in your compliments.

CAPTAIN: Yes, ma'am. I'll speak to you in all candor. I've always had an instinctive aversion to women, who are the natural enemies of the strength and dignity of man, as is shown by Eve, Armida,* that other scalawag who cut off Samson's hair, and many others that my cousin cites. But if there is anything that frightens me more than a woman, it's a lady, and especially a young, innocent, sensitive lady with dovelike eyes and rosy lips, with a figure like the serpent of Eden and a voice like a seductive siren, with small white hands like lilies that conceal tiger's claws and crocodile tears capable of deceiving and undoing all the saints in heaven. So my steadfast procedure has been to flee from all of you. Because, tell me: what arms does a man of my nature possess to deal with a twenty-year-old tyrant whose strength consists in her very weakness? Is it decorously possible to hit a woman? Of course not! So then, what recourse does a man have when he realizes that a very pretty and strong-willed snippet of a girl dominates him and controls him and keeps him constantly on edge?

ANGUSTIAS: You can do what I do when you say these funny and silly things to me. Be grateful for them and . . . smile! Because you've probably noticed that I'm not a weepy sort, for which reason the mention of crocodile tears in your portrait of the various "Angustiases" that—

CAPTAIN: Do you see? Not even Lucifer would come up with such a reply! Laugh at me is what you do all the time. Well, fine. I was saying, when you stabbed me in the back again, that of all the damsels I had feared encountering in the world, the most terrible, the most odious to a man of my temperament, forgive my frankness, is you. I don't ever remember having experienced the rage that I feel when you smile at seeing me furious. It seems to me that you're doubting my courage, the sincerity of my outbursts, the force of my character.

ANGUSTIAS: Then listen to me now and rest assured that I'm telling you the whole truth. I've already met many men out there, and although some have courted me I've not yet taken a fancy to any of them. But if I were to fall in love eventually, it would be with some wild Indian like you. You have a disposition that suits mine to a tee.

CAPTAIN: You can go straight to the devil! Countess! Doña Teresa! Call your daughter and tell her not to make my blood boil! Look: it's better that we not play *tute*. I realize that I can't cope with you. I've had several sleepless nights thinking about our arguments, about the harsh things you force me to say to you, about the irritating jokes with which you answer me, and about how impossible it is for you and me to live together in peace, in spite of how grateful I am to . . . to this house. Oh, I would have been better off if you had let me die in the middle of the street! It's a very sad thing to loathe and be unable to treat as is only fitting the person who has saved your life by risking hers. Fortunately, I'll soon be able to move this confounded leg, which means I can then go back to my little room on Calle de Tudescos, to the office of my seraphic relative and to my beloved casino, and this martyrdom will come to an end, this martyrdom to which you've condemned me with your face, your figure, your angelic acts, your coolness, your jokes, and your diabolic smile. We have only a few days left to be in each other's company. I'll come up with some way of continuing to keep in touch with your mother, alone, either at my cousin's house or through letters or by meeting her at some church or other. But as for you, my love, I won't go near you again until I know that you're married. What am I saying? Even less then! In short: leave me alone or tomorrow put toxin in my chocolate.

The day that Don Jorge de Córdoba spoke these words, Angustias did not smile but turned solemn and sad.

The captain noticed it and hastened to cover his face with the fold of the sheet, muttering to himself: "I've cut off my nose to spite my face by saying I don't want to play *tute*. But how can I take it back? I would disgrace myself. No, sir. Swallow hard, Captain Poison. Men must be men."

Angustias, who had already left the bedroom, did not learn of the regret and sadness that were floundering about underneath that bed linen.

III

Convalescence

WITH nothing of note to report, another fifteen days went by and then the big one arrived, the day on which our hero was to leave his bed, although with strict orders not to move from his chair and to keep the wounded leg extended on top of the other one.

Fully aware of it, the Marquis of Los Tomillares, who had every morning without fail visited Don Jorge—or rather, his adorable nurses, with whom he got along better than with his gruff and ill-tempered cousin—sent to the latter bright and early in the morning a magnificent chair-bed made of oak, steel, and damask, which he had had built well beforehand.

That luxurious piece of furniture was a consummate masterpiece, designed and superintended by the meticulous aristocrat. It had large wheels that facilitated moving the patient from one place to another; was operated by numerous cranks that converted it into either a folding bed or a reclining chair, with, in the latter position, a support for his right leg; and came equipped with a small table, bookrest, lapboard, mirror, and other detachable accessories, all admirably arranged.

To the ladies he sent, as he did every day, exquisite bouquets of flowers, and, in addition, as it was a special occasion, a huge selection of candies and a dozen bottles of champagne so that they could celebrate their guest's recovery. He presented the doctor with a beautiful watch and the servant with twenty-five *duros,* and with all of this, a veritable holiday was enjoyed in that house, in spite of the fact that the health of the respectable lady from Guipúzcoa was steadily failing.

The three women contended for the pleasure of wheeling the captain around in his chair-bed, and they all drank champagne and ate candy, both the sick and the healthy, even the representative of the medical profession. The marquis delivered a long pro-institution-of-marriage speech, and Don Jorge himself condescended to laugh several times, poking fun at his long-suffering cousin, and to sing "in public"—that is to say, in front of Angustias—a few verses of an Aragonese *jota.*

IV

Retrospective Glance

In truth, since the celebrated discussion of the fair sex, the captain had changed somewhat, if not in ways or manners, at least in disposition. And who's to say if not in ideas and sentiments too! One could see that skirts caused him less dread than in the beginning, and everybody had observed that the familiarity and kindness with which he treated Señora Barbastro were now having an effect on his relations with Angustias.

He continued, to be sure, and out of Aragonese obstinacy more than anything else, to declare himself her mortal enemy, and to speak to her with seeming sharpness, and loudly, as if he were issuing orders to soldiers, but his eyes followed her and settled on her with respect, and if by chance they crossed the increasingly more grave and sad expression of the intrepid and mysterious young woman, they seemed to inquire solicitously after that gravity and that sadness.

For her part, Angustias had stopped provoking the captain and smiling when she saw him raising his hackles. She would serve him in silence and in silence put up with his more or less sincere, bitter indifference until he too turned grave and sad and would ask with the openness of a good little boy: "What's the matter with you? Are you upset with me? Are you starting to pay me back for the abhorrence that I spoke to you about so much?"

"Let's drop the foolishness, Captain," she would reply. "Both of us have already engaged in too much of it while discussing serious matters."

"So you admit that you're retreating?"

"Retreating? From what?"

"Come, now! Surely you know. Didn't you tell me how brave and belligerent I was the day you called me a wild Indian?"

"And I don't regret it, my friend. But enough of this nonsense. I'll see you tomorrow."

"You're going? How can you? That's running away!"

"Whatever you say," Angustias replied, shrugging her shoulders. "But I'm leaving."

"And what am I supposed to do here alone all evening? Don't you see that it's only seven o'clock?"

"That's none of my affair. You can pray or sleep or talk to Mama. I have to continue putting my deceased father's trunk of papers in order. Why don't you ask Rosa for a pack of cards and play solitaire?"

"Be honest!" exclaimed the impertinent bachelor one day, devouring with his eyes his enemy's snow-white, dimpled hands. "Do you hold a grudge against me because we haven't played *tute* again since that morning?"

"Quite the contrary. I'm glad that we've given up that foolishness too," answered Angustias, hiding her hands in the pockets of her dressing gown.

"Well, then, dear girl, what do you want?"

"I don't want anything, Don Jorge."

"Why don't you call me 'Captain Poison' any more?"

"Because I realized that you don't deserve that name."

"You don't say! Have we resurrected sweetness and praise now? How do you know what I'm like on the inside?"

"I know that you would never poison a soul."

"Why not? Out of cowardice?"

"No, sir. Simply because you're an unfortunate man with a heart of gold that you have chained and gagged, whether from pride or fear of your own sensitivity, I don't know. And if this is not the case, let people ask my mother."

"Is that so? Let's change the subject. Keep your praise to yourself as you do your little ivory hands. This slip of a girl has decided to turn me inside out!"

"You would gain a great deal if I decided to do so and then indeed did it, since your *inside* is the *right side*. But that's neither here nor there. What do I have to do with your affairs?"

"Lord God Almighty! You could have asked yourself that question on the afternoon that you risked being shot to save my life!" exclaimed Don Jorge, and so forcefully that it seemed as though a bomb had exploded in his heart in place of gratitude.

Angustias looked at him contentedly and said with a noble fire in her voice: "I do not regret that act, because if I admired you a great deal when watching you fight on the afternoon of March 26th, I have admired you even more listening to you sing the *jota* while racked with pain, to distract and cheer up my poor mother."

"That's it! Make fun of my bad voice now!"

"Heavens, what a stubborn mule of a man! I'm not making fun of you, nor does the situation call for it. I've been on the verge of tears and blessed you from a distance every time that I heard you sing those verses."

"Tears! This is getting worse and worse. Ah, Señora Doña Angustias! One has to be very careful with you. You are determined to make me say ridiculous and absurd things that are unbecoming to a man of my character so that you can laugh at me afterward and declare yourself the victor. Fortunately I'm on my guard, and as soon as I see myself about to fall into your clutches, I'll start to run, broken leg and all, and won't stop until I'm halfway around the world. You must be what people call a coquette!"

"And you're a poor devil!"

"So much the better for me!"

"An unjust man, a barbarian, a fool!"

"That's it! Squeeze harder! This I like! For once we're going to fight!"

"An ingrate!"

"Not that, by George, not that!"

"Fine. But keep your gratitude to yourself because I, thank God, have no need of it whatsoever. And above all, please do not engage me again in another of these conversations."

So saying, Angustias turned her back on him, genuinely angry.

And thus there always remained, obscure and confused, the critical point that, unknowingly, these two souls were debating from the first time they laid eyes on each other . . . and that very soon was going to become as plain as day.

V

A Sudden Change

THE much anticipated and jubilant day on which Captain Poison got out of bed was to have an exceedingly mournful and lamentable end, a very frequent occurrence in the lives of human beings, as we noted philosophically in a previous chapter, but for reasons that were the direct opposite of the ones that follow.

Night was falling. The doctor and the marquis had just left, and Angustias and Rosa had also gone off, on the advice of the very pleased lady from Guipúzcoa, to say a prayer to the Virgin of El Buen Suceso, who at that time still had a church on the Puerta del Sol named after her, when the captain, whom they had put back to bed, heard the street bell ring and Doña Teresa open the peephole and ask: "Who is it?" Then he heard her say, opening the door: "How was I to expect that you would come at this hour? This way, please." And a man's voice exclaimed, trailing off into the interior rooms: "I'm very sorry, Señora. . . ."

The rest of the sentence was lost in the distance, and all was still for a few minutes, until footsteps sounded again and the same man could be heard talking, as though saying goodbye, "I do hope that you will get over this and calm down," and Doña Teresa replying, "Don't worry," after which the street door opened and closed and profound silence reigned in the house.

The captain realized that something disturbing had happened to the widow and even expected that she would come in and tell him about it, but upon seeing that it was not happening that way, he concluded that the matter probably fell into the category of domestic secrets and refrained from calling out to her in a loud voice, although he thought he heard her sigh in the adjoining hall.

At this point the street bell rang again, and Doña Teresa opened the door instantly, which confirmed that she had not moved a step since the caller's departure, and then Angustias could be heard asking and exclaiming the following: "Why were you waiting for us with your hand on the latch? Mama, what's wrong? Why are you crying? Why aren't you answering me? You're ill! God forbid! Rosa! Hurry and bring Dr. Sánchez! My mother's dying! Wait! First come here and help me carry her to the sofa in the drawing room! Don't you see that she's falling? My poor mother! My dear mother! What's the matter that you can't walk?"

It was true, she could not walk. Don Jorge, from his bedroom, saw Doña Teresa being practically dragged into the drawing room as she hung onto the necks of her daughter and the servant, her head drooped over her chest.

Angustias then remembered that the captain was in the world and, letting out a furious yell, she confronted him and asked: "What have you done to my mother?"

"No, no! The poor thing! He knows nothing!" the sick woman quickly said in a warm voice. "I got ill on my own. And I'm already starting to get over it."

The captain was red with indignation and shame. "Do you hear that, Señorita Angustias?" he finally asked in a very sad, bitter tone. "You've slandered me inhumanely! But, ah, no! I'm the one, I've slandered myself since I've been here! I deserve that kind of injustice from you.

"Doña Teresa," he continued, "don't pay any attention to this ingrate and tell me that you've recovered completely or I'll cash in my chips right here, where I'm tied down by pain and crucified by my enemy!"

Meanwhile, the widow had been made comfortable on the sofa and Rosa was crossing the street to summon the doctor.

"Forgive me, Captain," said Angustias. "Take into account that she is my mother and that I found her dying far from your side, where I left her fifteen minutes ago. Did someone come during my absence?"

The captain was going to answer "Yes," when Doña Teresa hurriedly replied: "No, no one. Isn't it true that no one came, Don Jorge? This is a question of nerves . . . dizzy spells . . . old age. Nothing more than old age. I'm all right now, my dear."

When the doctor arrived, he took the pulse of the widow

whom he had left a half hour ago in such a happy and nearly normal state, whereupon he said that she had to go to bed immediately and that she would have to stay in bed for some time—until there was a cessation of the acute nervous disturbance that she had just experienced. And moments later he informed Angustias and Don Jorge, in secret, that Doña Teresa's illness was cardiac in nature, and that he had had clear proof of it since taking her pulse for the first time on the afternoon of 26 March, and that such conditions, although not easy to cure completely, could be borne for a long time through rest, well-being, moderate happiness, good care, and who knows how many other wonders, the source of which was money.

"March 26th!" murmured the captain. "In other words, I'm to blame for everything that is happening."

"I am!" said Angustias, as though talking to herself.

"Don't go looking for the cause of causes," Dr. Sánchez sadly cautioned them. "In order for there to be blame it has to be preceded by intent, and both of you are incapable of having wanted to harm Doña Teresa."

The two pardoned listeners looked at each other with angelic surprise upon seeing that science was racking its brains to make such impious or such obvious inferences; and turning their attention at once to what really mattered to them then, they said to each other simultaneously: "She has to be saved!"

And that was their first step toward mutual understanding.

VI

Catastrophe

As soon as the doctor left, and after a long discussion, it was agreed that the widow's bed would be put in her boudoir, which, as we have already noted, was located at the other end of the drawing room, directly opposite the bedroom occupied by Don Jorge.

"This way," said the sensible Angustias, "our two charges can see and talk to each other, and it'll be easy for Rosa and me to look after both of you from the drawing room on the nights that we take turns sitting up with you."

That night, Angustias stayed with them and nothing unusual happened. Doña Teresa quieted down considerably near daybreak and dozed for about an hour. The doctor found her much improved the following morning, and, as she spent the day more and more comfortably, the second night Angustias withdrew to her room after two o'clock, giving in to her mother's tender entreaties and the captain's imperious orders, and Rosa stayed as the nurse, in the same armchair, in the same posture, and snoring the same as when she had stayed with the captain the night after he was wounded.

It was around three-thirty in the morning when our troubled hero, who was not asleep, heard Doña Teresa breathing with great difficulty and calling him in a muffled, faltering voice.

"Neighbor, are you calling me?" asked Don Jorge, masking his anxiety.

"Yes, Captain," the sick woman replied. "Awaken Rosa carefully, so that my daughter won't hear her. I can't speak any louder."

"But what's this? Do you feel ill?"

"Very ill. And I want to talk to you alone before I die. Have Rosa help you into the chair-bed and wheel you over here. But try to keep my poor Angustias from waking up."

The captain followed to the letter what Doña Teresa told him to do, and a few moments later he was at her side.

The poor widow had a very high fever and labored breathing. The indelible mark of death could easily be seen on her livid face.

The captain was terrified for the first time in his life.

"Leave us, Rosa, but don't awaken Señorita Angustias. God will want to let me live until daybreak, and then I'll call her so that we can say goodbye to each other.

"Listen, Captain. I'm dying."

"What do you mean you're dying?" responded Don Jorge,

clasping the sick woman's hand. "This is a passing discomfort, like the one yesterday afternoon. And besides, I don't want you to die!"

"I'm dying, Captain. I know it. It would be futile to summon the doctor. We'll summon my confessor, of course, even if it frightens my poor daughter. But that will be after you and I have finished talking, because what's urgent now is that the two of us talk without witnesses."

"Well, we are talking," said the captain, betraying his fear by smoothing his mustache. "Ask me for the little and poor blood with which I entered this house, and the ample and very rich blood that I've produced in it, and I shall gladly spill it all!"

"I know that, my friend, I know that. You are very honorable and think the world of us. And for this reason, my dear captain, I want you to know everything: yesterday afternoon my agent came and told me that the government had denied my petition for a widow's pension."

"Confound it! And you're fretting about that trifle? The government has denied any number of my petitions."

"I'm no longer a countess or a general's wife," the widow continued. "How right you were to use these titles sparingly with me!"

"So much the better! I'm not a general or a marquis either, and my grandfather was both. So we're on an equal footing."

"Fine, but the point is that I'm . . . I'm . . . completely ruined! My father and my husband spent all they had on behalf of the cause of Don Carlos. Until now I've lived off the sale of my jewelry, and eight days ago I sold the last piece, a beautiful pearl necklace. It makes me blush to talk to you about these unseemly considerations."

"Talk, Señora, talk! We've all suffered hardships. If you knew the binds I've been in on account of that confounded *tute!*"

"But there's no solution for my bind. All my resources and my daughter's entire fortune were pinned on that widow's pension, which with time would have been Angustias's orphan's pension. And today . . . the poor thing has no future, no present, and no money to bury me. Because—I want you to know this—the lawyer who was advising me, his pride hurt because my daughter had rejected him, or anxious to heighten our misfortune so as to bend Angustias's will and compel her to marry him, sent me last night the bill for his professional services at the same time as the disastrous news. The agent also presented me with his fee, and spoke to me in such a cruel fashion on behalf of the lawyer, mingling words like 'distrust,' 'insolvency,' 'attachment,' and I don't remember what others, that I went blind and, unseeing, pulled the drawer open and gave him all that he asked for, I mean, all that I had left, what I had been given for the pearl necklace, the last of my money, the last of my bread. And, therefore, since the night before last, Angustias is as poor as those wretches who beg from door to door. And she doesn't know it! She's sleeping peacefully at this moment. How, then, can I not be dying? The odd thing is that I didn't die the night before last."

"Well, don't die over such a small matter!" said the captain in a cold sweat, but with noble effusiveness. "You've done the right thing by talking to me. I'll make a sacrifice and live among skirts, like a dispenser of alms for nuns. It must be preordained! When I get well, instead of going back to my house, I'll have my clothes brought here, as well as my arms and my dogs, and we'll all live together until the end of time."

"Together!" the lady from Guipúzcoa exclaimed mournfully. "Didn't you hear me? Can't you see that I'm dying? Do you think I would have spoken to you about my financial problems if I wasn't certain that I would be dead within a few hours?"

"Then, Doña Teresa . . . what is it that you want from me?" asked Don Jorge de Córdoba, terrified. "Because it goes without saying that just to accord me the honor and pleasure of asking me, or entrusting me with asking my cousin, for that mere nothing called 'money,' you wouldn't be agonizing so much, knowing what a high regard we have for you and your daughter, and knowing us as I believe you know us. You'll never be in need of money while I'm alive! So there's something else that you want from me, and before you say another word I beg you to take into account the gravity of the circumstances and other considerations very worthy of attention."

"I don't understand you, nor do I myself know what I want," said Doña Teresa, with all the sincerity of a saint. "But put yourself in my place. I'm a mother. I adore my daughter. I'm going to leave her alone in the world. I have one foot in the grave and don't see a single person at my side, no one on the face of the earth, to whom I can entrust her, unless it be you, who, in spite of everything, shows a liking for her. To tell the truth, I don't know how you could help her. Money *alone* is so cold, so repugnant, so horrible! But it would be more horrible still if my poor Angustias had to earn a living with her hands, or become a servant, or beg! So I think it's justifiable, realizing that I'm dying, that I've called you to say goodbye and that, with my hands crossed and crying for the last time in my life, I should say to you, from the edge of the grave: 'Captain, be a guardian, be a father, be a brother to my poor orphan. Protect her. Help her. Defend her life and her honor. Don't let her die of hunger or sorrow. Don't let her be alone in the world. Imagine that a daughter has been born to you today.'"

"Thank God!" exclaimed Don Jorge, slapping the arms of the chair-bed with his palms. "I'll do that and much more for Angustias. But I sweated blood thinking that you were going to ask me to marry the girl."

"Señor Don Jorge de Córdoba! That's something no mother would ask! Nor would my Angustias tolerate my using her noble and brave heart!" said Doña Teresa with such dignity that a chill went down the captain's spine.

The poor man finally recovered and, kissing the dying woman's hands, held forth with the humility of a loving son: "Forgive me, Señora, forgive me! I'm a fool, a monster, an uneducated man who doesn't know how to explain himself. It was not my intention to offend you or Angustias. What I meant to say in good faith is that I would make that beautiful young woman, that model of virtue, very unhappy if I married her, and that I wasn't born to love or be loved, nor to live with another person, nor to have children, nor for anything that is sweet, tender, and affectionate. I'm independent like a savage, like a wild animal, and the yoke of marriage would humiliate me, drive me to despair, make me fly the coop. As for the rest, she neither loves me nor do I deserve her nor is there any reason to speak of this subject. On the other hand, please believe, on the strength of these first tears that I'm shedding since becoming a man and these first kisses from my lips, that everything I may earn in the world, as well as my concern and my vigilance and my blood, will be for Angustias, whom I respect and like and love, and to whom I owe my life, and perhaps even my soul. I swear by this holy medal that my mother always wore around her neck. I swear by. . . . But, you don't hear me! You're not answering me! You're not looking at me! Señora! Countess! Doña Teresa! Do you feel worse? Oh my God! I think she's dead! And here I am unable to move! Hang it all! Rosa! Rosa! Water! Vinegar! A confessor! A cross and I'll commend her soul as best I can! But I have my medal! Oh Most Blessed Virgin, receive my second mother into your bosom! Well, aren't I the calm one! Poor Angustias! Poor me! I've gotten myself into a real fix on account of hunting revolutionaries!"

All these exclamations were indeed apt. Doña Teresa had died upon feeling Captain Poison's kisses and tears on her hand, and a smile of supreme happiness still played on the half-open lips of her body.

VII

Miracles of Grief

At the dismayed guest's shouts, followed by the plaintive cries of the servant, Angustias awoke. She threw on some clothes, terror-stricken, and ran to her mother's boudoir. But she found the doorway closed off by Don Jorge's chair-bed, and Don Jorge himself, with his arms outstretched and his eyes bulging, blocking her way and saying: "Don't go in, Angustias! Don't go in or I'll get up even if it's the end of me!"

"My poor mother! My beloved mother! Let me see my

mother!" the poor thing wailed, struggling to go in.

"Angustias! In the name of God, don't go in now. We'll go in together later. Let the good woman who suffered so much rest for a moment."

"My mother has died!" exclaimed Angustias, falling on her knees next to the captain's chair-bed.

"My poor child! Cry with me as much as you want!"* said Don Jorge, drawing the poor orphan's head to his heart with one hand and caressing her head with the other one. "Cry with the man who had never cried until today, who cries for you . . . and for her!"

That emotion was so extraordinary and marvelous in a man like Captain Poison that Angustias, in the midst of her terrible misfortune, could not help but show her appreciation and gratitude by putting one of her hands over his heart.

And thus were those two souls locked in an embrace for a few moments, two souls whom happiness would never have made friends.

Part IV

From Strength to Strength

I

About How the Captain Came to Talk to Himself

FIFTEEN days after the funeral of Doña Teresa Carrillo de Albornoz, around eleven o'clock on a splendid morning of the month of flowers, a day or two before the feast of San Isidro,* our friend Captain Poison was striding quickly back and forth in the drawing room of the home of the deceased, supported by two beautiful ebony and silver crutches of unequal length, a gift from the Marquis of Los Tomillares; and although the pampered convalescent was there alone, and no one was in the boudoir or the bedroom, from time to time he would speak in a low voice, and with his customary fury and acerbity. "No, sir! No, sir! It's quite clear!" he finally exclaimed, stopping in the middle of the room. "Nothing can be done about it. I'm walking with perfect ease. And I even believe that I'd walk better without these sticks. Which means that I can go back to my house now."

At this point he let out a noisy breath, as though he were sighing in his own way, and murmured, changing his tone: "*I can!* I said *I can!* And what is *can*? Before, I used to think that a man could do anything he wanted to, and now I see that he cannot even want what suits him. Wily women! I've been right to fear this since the day I was born. And well did I know it as soon as I saw myself surrounded by skirts on

99

the night of March 26th. Your precaution came to naught, dear father of mine, when you arranged to have me nursed by a goat. After all these years, I've fallen into the hands of these despots who drove you to commit suicide. But, ah, I shall escape, even if I leave my heart in their claws!"

Next he glanced at the clock, sighed again, and said very quietly, as if conserving his strength: "A quarter after eleven and I still haven't seen her, although I've been up since six. What times those were, when she used to bring me my chocolate and we'd play *tute*! Now, whenever I call, the Galician responds. May 'so worthy a servant,' as my fool of a cousin would say, be no more! But on the other hand, it'll soon be twelve and they'll inform me that breakfast is served. I'll go to the dining room and there I'll meet a statue dressed in mourning that neither talks, nor laughs, nor cries, nor eats, nor drinks, a statue that knows nothing of what her mother told me that night, nothing of what is going to happen if God doesn't remedy the situation. The proud daughter believes that she's in her own home, and her sole concern is that I recover fully and depart so that my presence won't tarnish her reputation. The poor thing! How can I disabuse her? How can I tell her that I've deceived her, that her mother didn't give me any money, that for fifteen days everything that's been spent here has come out of my own pocket? Oh, never that! I'd rather die than tell her such a thing. But what can I do? How can I not give her a true or false account sooner or later? How can I go on this way indefinitely? She won't allow it. She'll take me to task when she calculates that I should have run out of what she imagines her mother possessed, and then there will be an ungodly row in this house."

Don Jorge de Córdoba's thoughts were taking this turn when a few light knocks were heard on the main door of the drawing room, followed by this question from Angustias: "May I come in?"

"Of course you may come in!" shouted the captain, beside himself with joy and hurrying to open the door while forgetting all his apprehensions and reflections. "It was about time you paid me a visit like before! You have a caged bear here, looking to pick a fight with someone. Do you want to play a hand of *tute*? But . . . what's the matter? Why are looking at me like that?"

"Let's sit down and talk, Captain," Angustias said gravely. And her bewitching face, pale as a ghost, expressed the deepest feeling.

Don Jorge twirled his mustache, as he always did whenever he sensed a storm brewing, and sat down on the edge of an armchair, glancing here and there with the air and uneasiness of a condemned criminal.

The young woman took a seat very close to him, reflected a few moments, or rather gathered strength for the imminent storm, and finally spoke with imponderable sweetness:

II

A Pitched Battle

"SEÑOR de Córdoba, the morning on which my blessed mother died, and when, yielding to your entreaties, I withdrew to my room after having laid her out, because you had insisted on remaining alone to watch by her bedside, with a respect and veneration that I shall never regret—"

"Come, now, Angustias! Keep your head! Put a fierce face to the enemy. Have the courage to overcome these things."

"You know I've not wanted for it until today," she said more calmly. "But I'm not referring now to this grief, with which I live and will live forevermore in holy peace, and whose sweet torment I would not surrender for anything in the world. I'm referring to problems of a different nature, which, fortunately, can be remedied, and are going to be completely remedied at once."

"God willing!" exclaimed the captain, seeing the storm cloud coming closer and closer.

"I was saying," continued Angustias, "that that morning you spoke to me more or less as follows: 'My child—'"

"You don't say! I called you 'My child!'"

"Let me continue, Don Jorge. 'My child!' you exclaimed in a tone of voice that affected me deeply. 'You don't have to think about anything except crying and praying to God for your mother. You know that I accompanied that holy woman in her last moments. That's why she made me privy to all her affairs and handed over to me all the money she had so that I could pay for the funeral, mourning clothes and other expenses as your guardian, which she designated me in private, and in order to spare you worries in the first days of your grief. When you get hold of yourself, we'll settle accounts.'"

"So what are you asking?" interrupted the captain, frowning deeply, as if by looking formidable he wished to change the reality of the situation. "Have I not fulfilled my responsibilities well? Have I done anything mad? Do you think I've squandered your inheritance? Was it not right to pay for a first-class funeral? Or perhaps you've already been told by some gossipmonger that I had a large headstone put on her grave with her titles of *Wife of General* and *Countess*? Well, the idea of the headstone was my personal whim, and I had intended to ask you to permit me to pay for it out of my own pocket. I couldn't resist the temptation of giving my noble friend the pleasure and the pomp of using among the dead the honorifics that were denied her by the living!"

"I didn't know about the headstone," Angustias uttered with heartfelt gratitude, taking and clasping one of Don Jorge's hands, despite his efforts to withdraw it. "God bless you! I accept that gift in my mother's and my name. But, even so, you were very wrong, very wrong indeed, to deceive me with respect to other points, and if I had learned of them sooner I would have come to ask you for an explanation sooner."

"And will it be possible to know, my dear young lady, in what way I've deceived you?" Don Jorge still dared to ask, not imagining that Angustias could know things that Doña Teresa had related only to him, and just moments before she passed away.

"You deceived me that sad morning," the young woman responded sternly, "when you told me that my mother had given you a certain amount—"

"And on what does her ladyship base herself to contradict with such cheek a prominent army captain, an honest man, an older person?" shouted Don Jorge with feigned vehemence, trying to interrupt noisily and kick up a row in order to get out of that tight situation.

"I base myself," Angustias calmly replied, "on the certainty, acquired afterwards, that my mother had no money when she fell ill."

"What do you mean 'no money?' These young things think they know it all! Then you're unaware that Doña Teresa had just disposed of a very valuable piece of jewelry?"

"No, that I knew. A pearl necklace with diamond brooches, for which she was given five hundred *duros*."

"Exactly. A necklace of pearls as big as walnuts, and we still have a lot of its value in gold left to spend. Do you want me to hand the money over to you right now? Do you wish to take charge already of the administration of your inheritance? Have you fared that badly under my guardianship?"

"What a good man you are, Captain! But what an imprudent one at the same time!" exclaimed the young woman. "Read this letter, which I've just received, and you'll see where those five hundred *duros* have been since the afternoon that my mother fell gravely ill."

The captain turned redder than a beet, but he still made a supreme effort and exclaimed, pretending to be furious: "So you're saying that I lie! So a scrap of paper carries more weight than I do! So lifelong integrity, with my word as good as that of a king, means nothing!"

"It means a great deal, Don Jorge, and I am deeply grateful that for me, and only for me, you have this one time broken that good custom."

"Let's see what the letter says!" the captain said in order to ascertain if he might find in it a way of mitigating the situation. "It'll probably be nonsense."

The letter was from the lawyer or adviser of the general's deceased wife and read as follows:

Señorita Doña Angustias Barbastro

My dear lady and esteemed friend:

I have just received unofficially the sad news of the demise of your distinguished mother (May she rest in peace) and I accompany you in your understandable grief, wishing you the physical and moral strength to bear such an irremediable and hard blow from the higher authority that governs human destinies.

Having said this, which is not a mere oratorical formula of politeness, but an expression of the old and stated affection that my soul professes for you, I have to fulfill another sacred duty by you, and it is as follows:

Your deceased mother's business agent, upon giving me the painful news, told me that when, two weeks ago, he went to inform her of the unfavorable outcome of her petition for a widow's pension and to present to her the bills for our services, he had occasion to appreciate that Doña Teresa scarcely possessed sufficient money to discharge them, as she unfortunately did do then and there, with a haste in which I discerned new signs of the bitter dislike which you too had shown for me previously.

Now, then, my dear Angustias: I am considerably tormented by the idea that you may be suffering hardship and deprivation in such dire circumstances on account of the excessive speed with which your mother paid that sum (a reduced fee for the six petitions, whose first draft I wrote and of which I even made a fair copy), and I beg your prior consent to return the money, and even to add however much more you may need and I possess.

I cannot help it if I do not have sufficient personality or other qualities except a love that is as great as it is unreciprocated upon making you such an offer, which I beg you to accept in due form from your fervent admirer and attentive friend.

Most respectfully and obediently yours,

Tadeo Jacinto de Pajares

"Now there's a lawyer whose neck I'm going to wring!" exclaimed Don Jorge, raising the letter above his head. "That scoundrel! That skinflint! That swine! He hastens the good woman's death by talking to her of 'insolvency' and 'attachment' when asking for payment to see if he could force her to give him your hand, and now he wants to buy that same hand with the money he received from her for having lost the claim to the widow's pension. No, no! I'm paying him a little visit! Hand me those crutches. Rosa! My hat! I mean, go to my house and have them give it to you or, if not, bring me my forage cap, which should be in the bedroom. And the saber. But no, don't bring the saber. The crutches will be more than enough to knock his block off."

"Leave us, Rosa, and don't pay any attention to Don Jorge's jokes," said Angustias, tearing the letter to pieces. "And you, Captain, sit down and listen to me, I beg of you. I despise that lawyer with all his ill-gotten gains, and haven't answered him nor do I intend to. He's a coward and a miser and believed naturally that he could make a woman like me his simply by presenting our thin case for nothing in government offices. Let's not talk any more—not now, not ever—about that contemptible old man."

"Then let's not talk about anything else either," added the shrewd captain, managing to reach his crutches and beginning to walk quickly back and forth, as if he were fleeing from the interrupted discussion.

"But, my friend," the young woman said in a heartfelt tone, "things can't stay the way they are."

"All right! All right! We'll talk about that presently. The thing to do now is have breakfast because I'm famished. And how strong my leg feels thanks to that old fox of a doctor! I'm as good as new. Tell me, sweetheart, how do we stand today?"

"Captain!" exclaimed Angustias angrily. "I will not budge from this chair until you hear me out and we settle the matter that brought me here!"

"What matter? Come, now! Am I going to hear the same old refrain? And speaking of refrains, I swear to you that I will never again in my life sing the Aragonese *jota.* Poor countess!

How she used to laugh while listening to me!"

"Señor de Córdoba!" persisted Angustias with increasing bitterness. "I beg you again to pay some attention to a matter in which my honor and dignity are compromised."

"As far as I'm concerned you are not compromised in any way at all!" responded Don Jorge, brandishing the shorter of his crutches like a foil. "As far as I'm concerned you are the most honorable and dignified woman that God has created!"

"It's not enough to be one for you! It's necessary that everybody have the same opinion. So sit down and listen to me or I'll send for your cousin, who, as a man of conscience, will put an end to the shameful situation in which I find myself."

"I'm telling you I won't sit down. I'm fed up with beds, armchairs, and seats. Nevertheless, you may talk as much as you please," said Don Jorge, who had stopped brandishing his crutch but stayed on guard.

"I'll say very little to you," continued Angustias in the same grave tone, "and what little it is . . . must have occurred to you from the very beginning. Captain, you've been supporting this house for fifteen days. You paid for my mother's funeral; you paid for my mourning clothes; you've paid for the bread I've eaten. I cannot repay you at the moment what you've spent thus far, as I shall with time. But I want you to know that from this day forward—"

"Hell's fire, woman! *You* pay me? *She* pay me?" shouted the captain with as much distress as fury, raising his crutches on high until reaching the ceiling with the longer one. "This woman has set out to do me in! And it's for this that she wants me to listen to her! Well, I won't listen to you! The discussion is over. Rosa! Breakfast! Señorita, I shall await you in the dining room. Please do not be long in coming."

"What a fine way you have of respecting my mother's memory! How well you carry out the responsibilities she entrusted to you on behalf of this orphan! Some interest you're taking in my honor and peace of mind!" exclaimed Angustias with such majesty that Don Jorge checked himself like a horse that is reined in. He contemplated the young woman for a moment, flung the crutches far away from him, sat down again in the armchair, and said, folding his arms: "Talk until you're blue in the face!"

"I was saying," continued Angustias as soon as she had composed herself, "that from this day forward there will be an end to the absurd situation created by your imprudent generosity. You are well now and can move back to your house—"

"A fine arrangement!" interrupted Don Jorge, who immediately covered his mouth as if sorry for the interruption.

"The only one possible!" exclaimed Angustias.

"And then what will you do, for heaven's sake?" shouted the captain. "Live on air like chameleons?"

"What will I . . .? Well, I suppose I'll sell most of the furniture and draperies—"

"Which aren't worth a plugged nickel!" interrupted Don Jorge again, glancing scornfully at the four walls of the room, which were not very bare, the truth be told.

"For whatever they're worth," said the orphan gently. "The point is that I'll stop living at your expense, or off your cousin's charity."

"No, not that! God forbid! My cousin hasn't paid for a thing!" roared the captain with the utmost nobility. "That would be the last straw, with me still alive and kicking! It's true that poor Álvaro, because I want to give him credit where credit is due, offered to stand good for everything when he heard the terrible news, and by that I mean for much, much more than you could imagine. But I told him that the Countess of Santurce's daughter could only accept favors—or rather, grant them by the mere acceptance of them—from her guardian, Don Jorge de Córdoba, to whose care the deceased entrusted her. He saw that I was in the right, and then all I did was borrow from him, just borrow, a few *maravedises* against the salary that I earn as his steward. Consequently, Señorita Angustias, you can set your mind at ease on that score, even though you're as proud as a peacock."

"It's all the same to me," stammered the young woman, "since I'll have to pay back one of you when—"

"When what? That's the crux of the matter! Tell me when."

"When . . . when I've worked for a time, and with the help of a merciful God, to make my way in life—"

"Way? Way? What way?" shouted the captain. "Come, now, Angustias, don't talk nonsense. You work? Work with those pretty hands that I never tired of looking at when we used to play *tute*? Well, how come I'm in the world if the daughter of Doña Teresa Carrillo, my only friend, has to take up needle-work or ironing or the devil knows what else to earn a living of sorts?"

"Let's leave all of that up to me and to time," replied Angustias, lowering her eyes. "But meanwhile we agree that you will do me the favor of leaving today. That is true, is it not?"

"Stop your harping! And why does it have to be true? Why do I have to leave if things aren't going badly for me here?"

"Because you're well now, because you can walk out in the street now the same as you walk through the house, and it doesn't look good for us to continue living together."

"Then imagine that this is a boardinghouse. There! That settles it! This way you won't have to sell furniture or anything else. I'll pay you my room and board and you and Rosa can take care of me . . . and that's that! With my two salaries I make more than enough for all of us to get along very well, since in the future I won't be brought up on charges of disrespect, nor will I lose anything again at *tute*, unless it be my patience . . . whenever you beat me too many games in a row. Are we agreed?"

"You must be mad, Captain!" exclaimed Angustias in a melancholy voice. "You didn't enter this house as a boarder, nor would anyone believe that you were here in such a capacity, nor do I want you to be. I'm neither at the age nor in a position to run a boardinghouse. I prefer to earn a day's wage by sewing or embroidering."

"And I prefer to be hanged!" shouted the captain.

"You're very compassionate," continued the orphan, "and I thank you from the bottom of my heart for what you're suffering because you see that there is nothing you can do to help me. But that's life, that's the world, that's the law of society."

"What does society matter to me?"

"It matters a great deal to me! Among other reasons because its laws are a reflection of the law of God."

"So it's the law of God that I can't support whomever I please."

"Yes, Captain, it is, for the simple reason that society is divided into families—"

"I don't have a family, and consequently I can dispose of my money as I see fit."

"But I shouldn't accept it. The daughter of an honorable man whose name was Barbastro, and of an honorable woman whose name was Carrillo, cannot live at the expense of just anybody."

"Then for you I'm an 'anybody.'"

"And an anybody of the worst kind, since we're talking about my situation, and you are single, still young, and do not exactly have the reputation of a saint."

"Now look here, Señorita!" exclaimed the captain resolutely after a brief pause, like someone who is going to summarize and resume an involved controversy. "On the night that I helped your mother die in peace, I told her honestly and with my habitual candor—so that the good woman would not die with false hopes, but with full knowledge of what was happening—that I, Captain Poison, would go through anything in this world except have a wife and children. Do you want it more clearly?"

"What are you telling me?" Angustias asked with as much dignity as amusement. "Do you by some chance think that I'm indirectly asking you for your lily-white hand?"

"No, Señorita!" Don Jorge hurriedly answered, turning as red as a beet. "I know you too well to think such an absurd thought. Besides, we've already seen that you scorn millionaire suitors, like that lawyer of the famous letter. But what am I saying? Doña Teresa herself gave me the same answer as you when I disclosed to her my unshakable determination to never marry. However, I'm speaking to you about this so that you won't find it odd or be offended by the fact that—holding you in the regard that I do, and caring for you as I do . . . because I care for you a great deal more than you imagine—I don't take the bull by the horns and say: 'Enough beating around the bush, my darling. Let's get married and be done with it!'"

"Except that it wouldn't be enough for you to say it," the young woman answered with heroic coolness. "It would also be necessary for me to like you."

"Is that so?" roared the captain, jumping to his feet. "Then can it be that you don't like me?"

"And where do you come up with such a probability, Don Jorge?" retorted an implacable Angustias.

"Don't bring up probabilities or other kinds of nonsense!" thundered Mars's poor disciple. "I know what I'm talking about. What's happening here, to put it plainly, is that I can't marry you, nor live in any other way in your company, nor abandon you to your sad fate. But believe me, Angustias, you are neither a stranger to me nor am I one to you, and if I learned that you were earning that daily wage, that you were in service in some house, that you were working with your little pearly hands, that you were hungry or cold or—good Lord, I don't even want to think about it!—I would set fire to Madrid or blow my brains out. Compromise, then, and since you won't accept our living together like brother and sister, because the world smears everything with its contemptible thoughts, let me give you an annual allowance like the ones given by kings and queens and rich men to persons worthy of protection and help."

"But you, Don Jorge, are neither rich nor a king."

"But you are a queen to me, and I ought to and want to pay you the voluntary tribute with which loyal subjects usually support exiled monarchs."

"Enough of kings and queens, Captain," said Angustias with the sad, dignified calmness of despair. "You are not, nor can you be, anything but a very good friend from better times, whom I shall always remember with fondness. Let's say goodbye to each other, and leave me at least my dignity in my misfortune."

"Fine! And in the meantime I'll see the world through rose-colored glasses, knowing that the woman who saved my life by risking her own is going through hell. I'll have the satisfaction of thinking about the fact that the only daughter of Eve that I've ever liked, that I've ever cared for, that . . . I adore with my whole heart, is going without necessities, working to eat miserably, living in an attic, and not receiving any help, any solace from me—"

"Captain!" interrupted solemnly Angustias. "Men who cannot marry and who have the honesty to acknowledge it and proclaim it should not talk of adoration to honorable young ladies. So I repeat: send for a carriage, let's say good-bye to each other like decent people, and you'll hear from me when my life takes a turn for the better."

"Good God! What a woman this Angustias is!" the captain exclaimed, covering his face with his hands. "I was right to fear everything from the moment I laid eyes on her! There was a reason I stopped playing *tute* with her! There was a reason I spent so many sleepless nights! Has there ever been a predicament like mine? Yet how can I marry her after all the abuse I've heaped on matrimony? What would they say about me at the casino? What would be said by people who met me in the street arm-in-arm with a wife, or at home, feeding pap to a baby? Children and me? Me struggling with kids? Me hearing them cry? Me afraid all the time that they're sick, that they're dying, that they're being carried off? Angustias, as God is my witness, I was not born for these things. I would be in such despair that, to avoid seeing me and hearing me, you would cry out for a divorce or to be a widow. Take my advice. Don't marry me even though I may want you to."

"But, Don Jorge," said the young woman, leaning back in her armchair with admirable calm. "You're doing all the talking. Where do you get the idea that I want us to marry, that I would accept your offer, that I don't prefer to live alone, even if to do so I may have to work night and day as do other orphans?"

"You ask where I get the idea?" replied the captain with the greatest ingenuousness imaginable. "From the nature of things! From the fact that we both love each other! From the fact that we both need each other! From the fact that there is no other arrangement for a man like me and a woman like you to live together! Do you think that I don't know it, that I hadn't already thought about it, that your honor and good name are indifferent to me? But I've talked to talk, to run away from my own conviction, to see if I could escape the terrible dilemma that robs me of my sleep, and if I could find a way of not marrying you, as in the end I shall have to do, if you insist on living alone."

"Alone! Alone!" repeated Angustias wittily. "And why not with someone else? Who says that down the road I won't find a man to my liking who doesn't have an aversion to marriage?"

"Angustias! Let's change the subject!" shouted the captain, turning the color of sulfur.

"Why change it?"

"Let's change it, I said. And know from this moment forward that I'll eat the heart out of the foolhardy fellow who courts you. But it's wrong of me to get upset without any reason. I'm not so foolish that I don't realize what's happening to us. Do you want to know what that is? Well, it's very simple. We love each other. And don't tell me that I'm mistaken because that would be disregarding the truth. And here is the proof: if you didn't love me I wouldn't love you! What I'm doing is paying back, and I owe you so much. After having saved my life, you've attended me like a sister of Charity; you've endured patiently all the outrageous things that, to escape your seductive power, I've said to you for the better part of two months; you cried in my arms when your mother died; and you've been putting up with me now for an hour. In a word, Angustias, let's compromise and split the difference. Give me ten years. When I reach the half century mark and I'm another man, sick, old, and accustomed to the idea of slavery, we'll get married without anyone knowing it, and we'll leave Madrid to live in the country, where there are no people, where nobody can poke fun at the former Captain Poison. But, in the meantime, please accept in the strictest confidence, without a living soul learning about it, half of my earnings. You'll live here and I'll live in my house. We'll see each other, but always in front of witnesses, like at some formal social gathering. We'll write to each other every day.

I'll never walk up and down this street so as to avoid gossip and scandal, and, only on All Saints' Day, we'll go to the cemetery together, with Rosa, to visit Doña Teresa."

Angustias could not help but smile upon hearing the good captain's supreme speech. And that smile was not mocking, but joyful, like an ardently desired ray of hope, like the first reflection of the tardy star of happiness that was nearing her horizon. But a woman in the end, although as worthy and sincere as the best of them, who was able to repress her nascent joy, she said with feigned distrust, and with a firmness peculiar to a truly chaste reserve: "I can only laugh at the extravagant conditions that you set on granting your unsolicited wedding ring. You are cruel in denying alms to the needy person who has the arrogance not to beg, and who would not accept them for anything in the world. And keep in mind that right now we're talking about a young woman, neither ugly nor shameless, whom you've been rejecting for an hour as if she had wooed you. Therefore, let's put an end to this odious conversation, but not without my forgiving you, and even thanking you for your good, albeit ill-expressed, intentions. Shall I call Rosa now to have her go out for a carriage?"

"Not yet, you stubborn woman! Not yet!" replied the captain, standing up with a very thoughtful air about him, as though he were trying to give shape to a delicate, abstruse thought. "Another kind of compromise occurs to me, and this will be the last one. Do you understand, my lady with Aragonese blood? The last one that this other Aragonese will allow himself to propose to you. But to do so, first I need for you to answer a question honestly . . . after you hand me my crutches so that I can leave without saying another word in the event that you refuse to go along with what I intend to propose to you."

"Ask and propose," said Angustias, handing him his crutches with indescribable charm.

Don Jorge leaned, or rather, straightened up on them, and, fixing a searching, unyielding, imposing stare on the young woman, questioned her with the voice of a judge: "Do you like me? Do I seem acceptable to you, once I'm rid of these sticks which I'll soon throw away? Do we have a basis for discussion? Would you marry me immediately if I decided to ask you for your hand, under the abovementioned condition which I'll then explain to you?"

Angustias realized that she was gambling all to win all, but . . . even so, she got to her feet and said with her never disputed courage: "Don Jorge, that question is an insult, and no gentleman asks it of women he considers ladies. Enough of these absurdities already. Rosa! Rosa! Don Jorge de Córdoba is calling you."

And, having thus spoken, the magnanimous young woman headed for the main door of the room, after bowing coldly to the diabolical captain.

But the latter cut her off halfway there, thanks to the longer of his crutches, which he extended horizontally to the wall, like a gladiator who is floundering, and then he exclaimed with unwonted humility: "Don't leave, in memory of her who's watching us from heaven! I resign myself to your not answering my question and move on to propose the compromise. It must be preordained that only what you want will be done. But you, Rosita, leave as fast as your legs will carry you because you're not needed here!"

Angustias, who was struggling to remove the barrier that blocked her way, stopped upon hearing the captain's deeply felt plea, and stared him in the eye, without turning more than her head, and with an indefinable air of imperiousness, seduction, and impassivity. Never had Don Jorge seen her so beautiful or so expressive! Then she did indeed look like a queen!

"Angustias," continued saying, or rather, stammering, that hero of a hundred battles, with whom the young Madrilenian woman had fallen so much in love upon seeing him lead the charge like a lion in the midst of hundreds of bullets, "under one unchangeable, express condition of cardinal importance I have the honor of asking you for your hand so that we can get married whenever you say . . . tomorrow . . . today . . . as soon as we can arrange the papers . . . as quickly as possible, because I can't live without you!"

The young woman softened her look, and began to reward

Don Jorge for that true heroism with a delightful, tender smile.

"But I repeat that it's under one condition," the poor man hastened to add, realizing that Angustias's look and smile were beginning to drive him crazy and make him go weak at the knees.

"Under what condition?" she asked him with a bewitching calm, turning toward him completely and fascinating him with the flood of light from her black eyes.

"Under the condition," stammered the catechumen, "that if we have children we put them in the foundling hospital. Oh! On this I will never yield. Do you accept? Say yes, for heaven's sake!"

"Of course I accept, Captain Poison!" Angustias answered, laughing heartily. "You yourself will take them there. What am I saying? The two of us will go together. And we'll leave them there without kissing them or anything. Jorge! Do you think we'll take them there?"*

Thus did Angustias reply, looking at Don Jorge de Córdoba with angelic bliss.

The poor captain thought that he was dying of happiness; a river of tears sprang from his eyes and he exclaimed, wrapping his arms around the charming orphan: "So I'm lost!"

"Altogether lost, Captain Poison!" replied Angustias. "Therefore, let's have breakfast and then we'll play *tute*. In the afternoon, when your cousin comes, we'll ask him if he wants to be best man at our wedding, something that the good marquis has been hoping for, in my view, since the first time that he saw us together."

III

*Etiamsi Omnes**

ONE morning in the month of May 1852, that is, four years after the scene that we have just described, a certain friend of ours, the same one who told us this story, stopped his horse at the door of an old house that looked like a palace, on the Carrera de San Francisco in Madrid; he handed the reins to the lackey who accompanied him and asked the walking frock coat who met him at the doorway: "Is Don Jorge de Córdoba in his office?"

"The gentleman," the questioned piece of cloth answered in his Asturian dialect, "is inquiring, I assume, after His Excellency the Marquis of Los Tomillares."

"What? My dear Jorge is a marquis now?" responded the dismounted rider. "So good old Don Álvaro finally died? Don't be surprised that I didn't know, because I just returned last night after an absence of a year and a half."

"His Excellency Don Álvaro," said the servant solemnly, removing the baking pan trimmed with braid that he wore as a cap, "passed away eight months ago, leaving as his one and only heir his cousin and former steward, Don Jorge de Córdoba, the present Marquis of Los Tomillares."

"Well then, do me the favor of having someone inform him that his friend T——— is here."

"Go on up, sir. You will find him in the library. His Excellency does not like for us to announce visitors. He would rather we let everyone come in as if they owned the place."

"Fortunately," the visitor said to himself, climbing the stairs, "I know this house like the back of my hand, even though I don't own the place. So he's in the library, is he? Who would have thought that Captain Poison would turn into a scholar?"

When the person in question had gone through several rooms, meeting along the way other servants who simply said, "The master's in the library," he finally reached its storied door, opened it without knocking, and just stood there, astonished upon seeing the scene before him.

In the middle of the carpeted room was a man on all fours; mounted on top of his back was a little boy about three years old, spurring him with his heels, while another little boy, about a year and a half, who had planted himself in front of the man's disheveled head, was pulling him by his necktie, as if it were a halter, and saying thickly: "Giddyap, horsey!"

The End

Moors and Christians

I

THE once famous but now little known town of Aldeire forms a part of the marquisate of El Cenet, or, as it were, the backside of the Alpujarra's* eastern flank, and is half-suspended, half-hidden in a gorge or ravine of the huge central mass of the Sierra Nevada, five or six thousand feet above sea level and six or seven thousand beneath the eternal snows of the Mulhacén.*

Aldeire, let it be said with the forgiveness of its parish priest, is a Moorish town. That it was once Moorish is clearly proclaimed by its name, its location, and its architecture; and that it has not yet become entirely Christian, even though it figures as such in reconquered Spain* and has its little Catholic church and its confraternities of the Virgin, of Jesus, and of a goodly number of saints of both sexes, is confirmed by the character and customs of its inhabitants, by the passions, terrible and chimerical in equal parts, that unite or separate them in perpetual bands, and by the somber black eyes, pale complexion, and scant speech and laughter of men, women, and children.

Because it would be well to point out, so that neither the abovementioned priest nor anyone else can question the soundness of this reasoning, that the Moors of the marquisate of El Cenet were not expelled in a body as were those of the Alpujarra; on the contrary, many of them managed to remain there, hidden and holed up thanks to the prudence or cowardice with which they turned a deaf ear to the reckless and heroic cry of their ill-starred prince, Aben-Humeya.* Wherefore I deduce that Uncle Juan Gómez, alias the Ant, constitutional mayor of Aldeire in the year of grace 1821, could very well have been a descendant of some Mustafa, Muhammad, or the like.

In any event, the story goes that this Juan Gómez, at the time upwards of fifty, a very astute although illiterate peasant, and greedy and fruitfully industrious, as attested to not only by his nickname but also by his wealth, which he had acquired by hook or by crook and invested in the choicest real estate of the district, this Juan Gómez, for next to nothing, the result of a gift of several nonlaying hens that he had given to the secretary of the town council, took out a perpetual lease from among community property holdings on a tract of unirrigated land at the outskirts of the town, in the middle of which could be seen the remains and debris of an ancient framework, hermitage, or Moorish watchtower, which was still called the Moor's Tower.

Needless to say, Uncle Ant did not stop to reflect even for an instant on who that Moor might have been, nor on the nature or original purpose of the ruined structure. The only thing that he saw immediately, as plain as day, was that with so many already fallen stones, and others that he would knock down, he could erect there a handsome and very secure corral for his livestock. So the very next day, as a diversion in keeping with someone as parsimonious as he, Juan Gómez devoted his afternoons to demolishing, by himself and alone, what still stood of the venerable Moorish tower.

"You're going to kill yourself!" his wife would say when she saw him coming back at night covered with dust and sweat, hiding the crowbar under his cloak.

"On the contrary!" he would reply. "This exercise is just the ticket for me not to waste away like our sons the students, who, according to what the tobacconist told me, were at the theater in Granada the other night with such pasty faces that it turned your stomach to look at them."

"The poor things! It's from so much studying! But you, you ought to be ashamed to work like a common laborer, being as you are the richest man in the town, and mayor to boot."

"Which is why I go by myself. Come on now. Pass me that salad."

"Nonetheless, it would be worth your while to have someone help you. It's going to take you forever to knock down the tower, and at that you may not find a way to raze it completely."

"Don't talk nonsense, Torcuata. When the time comes to build the corral wall, I'll take on day laborers, and I'll even bring in a master mason. But knock it down—anyone can do that! And it's so much fun to destroy! Anyway, clear the table and let's go to bed."

"You're saying that because you're a man. I see it differently: everything involving destruction scares me and troubles me."

"An old woman's weakness. If you knew how many things in this world ought to be destroyed!"

"Hold your tongue, you Freemason! It was a dark day when you were elected mayor. You watch, when the Royalists* return to power, the absolute king will hang you."

"As for that . . . we'll see. Hypocritical woman! Sanctimonious woman! Owlish woman! All right, put that light out and stop making the sign of the cross because I'm very sleepy."

II

ONE afternoon Uncle Ant returned from his labors in a very preoccupied, pensive mood, and earlier than usual.

His wife waited until he sent the workers on their way to ask him what was wrong, and by way of an answer he showed her a lead tube with a lid, much the same as the ones carried by soldiers on leave. From it he removed, and carefully unrolled, a yellow parchment written in unintelligible characters, and said with impressive solemnity: "I don't know how to read, not even in Spanish, which is the clearest language in the world, but I'll eat my hat if this isn't the writing of a Moor."

"So you're saying you found it in the tower?"

"I'm not saying it only for that reason, but because these hen tracks don't look like anything I've seen scrawled by Christians."

Juan Gómez's wife eyed and sniffed the parchment and exclaimed with a certainty as comical as it was groundless: "It's the writing of a Moor all right! And even though I don't know how to read either, I would swear that we have in our hands the discharge of some soldier of Muhammad who is now in the depths of hell."

"Are you saying so on account of the lead tube?"

"I'm saying so on account of the lead tube."

"Well, you're totally mistaken, my dear Torcuata, because the Moors, as our son Agustín has told me a number of times, didn't have conscription. So this isn't a discharge. This is the . . . the. . . ." Uncle Ant glanced around, lowered his voice, and said with absolute certainty: "This is the key to a treasure!"

"You're right!" agreed his wife, inflamed all of a sudden with the same belief. "And have you already found it? Is it very big? Were you careful to hide it again? Are the coins silver or gold? Do you think they're still in circulation? What happiness for our sons! How they're going to spend and celebrate in Granada and Madrid! I want to see it! Take me there! The moon's out tonight!"

"Good heavens, woman! Calm down! How do you expect me to have come across the treasure by following these scribbles if I don't know how to read in Moorish or Christian?"

"That's true! Well, look, what you can do is saddle a good mule at daybreak, cross the sierra by way of the Ragua Pass, which is supposed to be safe, and go to Ugíjar, to the house of our *compadre** Don Matías de Quesada, who, as you know, understands everything. He'll clear up this matter and give you sound advice, as usual."

"All his advice costs me a tidy sum, in spite of our kinship. But I too had thought of the same thing. Tomorrow I'll go to

Ugíjar and be back by nightfall if I push the mule a little."

"But make sure that you explain things to him fully."

"There isn't much to explain. The tube was hidden in an opening or niche in the thickest part of the wall, and covered with tiles like the ones from Valencia. I demolished the entire partition and didn't find anything else of interest. Underneath it is anchored the masonry of the foundation, whose enormous stones more than a yard square could be removed by two or three men as strong as I am, but only with difficulty. Consequently, we need to know for certain where the treasure was hidden, otherwise we'll have to rip out all the foundations of the tower with our neighbors' help."

"No, no! Leave for Ugíjar as soon as day breaks. Offer our *compadre* a share, but not a very large one, of whatever we find, and when we know where we have to dig, I'll help you myself to rip out the stonework. My precious sons! It'll all be for them! As for me, my one concern is that there might be a sin in this scheme that we're hatching under our breaths."

"What sin can there be, you simpleton?"

"I don't know how to explain it to you, but treasures have always seemed to me like something associated with the devil, or with fairies. Besides, you leased that piece of land for such a low annual payment. The whole town says there was skullduggery in that business."

"That has to do with the secretary and the councilors. They drew up the document for me."

"Moreover, I understand that with treasures one must give a share to the king."

"That's when they're not discovered on one's own land, and this site is mine."

"One's own! One's own! I wonder to whom that tower that the town council sold you really belonged."

"Well, to the Moor!"

"And I wonder who that 'Moor' could have been! At any rate, Juan, whatever money he might have hidden in his house would be his or his heirs, not yours or mine."

"You're talking nonsense! By that reasoning I shouldn't be the mayor of Aldeire—the mayor should be the one who held office last year when Riego rose in revolt.* By that reasoning we would have to send to the Moors' descendants in Africa, every year, the income generated by the plains of Granada and Guadix and hundreds of other towns."

"You may be right. In any event, go to Ugíjar, and our *compadre* will advise you as best he can regarding this matter."

<h1 style="text-align:center">III</h1>

UGÍJAR is about twelve very arduous miles from Aldeire. Nevertheless, it had not even struck nine o'clock the following morning when Uncle Juan Gómez, wearing his blue knitted knee breeches and his embroidered white Sunday boots, arrived at the office of Don Matías de Quesada, a hale and hearty man of ripe old age, a doctor in both civil and criminal law and advocate of the redress of the greater part of the wrongs committed at that time in that part of the country. All his life he had been a litigious attorney, and in addition to being worth a fortune he was very well connected in Granada and Madrid.

When he had heard his worthy *compadre's* story, and after he had carefully examined the parchment, he said that, in his opinion, nothing in it smelled of a treasure; that the niche in which he found the tube must have been where babouches were kept; and that the writing looked to him like a kind of prayer that Moors usually say every Friday morning. But, nonetheless, he also said that, as he was not all that well versed in Arabic, he would send the document to Madrid, to a classmate of his who was employed in the Office of Holy Places, so that he could send it on to Jerusalem to be translated into Spanish, to which end it would be fitting to remit to the Madrilenian a bank draft for a couple of ounces of gold, for a cup of chocolate.

Uncle Juan Gómez deliberated for a long time before deciding to pay for such a costly cup of chocolate (which would amount to 10,240 *reales* per pound); but so certain was he with regard to the "treasure" (and in truth he was not mistaken, as we'll see in due course), that he took from his sash eight small coins, each worth twenty pesetas, and handed them over to the attorney, who weighed them one by one before pocketing them. This done, Uncle Ant headed back to Aldeire, determined to continue excavating the Moor's Tower, while the parchment was being sent to the Holy Land, translated, and returned, steps which, according to the counselor, would take approximately a year and a half.

IV

No sooner had Uncle Juan turned his back than his *compadre* and adviser picked up his pen and wrote the following, beginning with the envelope:

SEÑOR DON BONIFACIO TUDELA Y GONZÁLEZ, Choirmaster of the Holy Cathedral Church of Ceuta.*

My dear nephew-in-law:

Only to a man of your righteousness would I entrust the momentous secret contained in the attached document. I say so because beyond a doubt written herein are the keys to a treasure, of which I shall give you a portion if I succeed in discovering it with your help. To this end, it is imperative that you find a Moor to translate the parchment, and that you send me the translation by certified letter without mentioning the matter to a soul, unless it be your wife, whom I know to be a discreet person.

Forgive my not having written to you in so many years, but you know full well that I have a lot to do. Your aunt continues to pray for you every night before going to bed. I hope you have recovered from the stomach ailment you were suffering in 1806.

Love,

Matías de Quesada
Your uncle-in-law

Ugíjar, 15 January 1821

P.S. Regards to Pepa, and let me know if you've had children.

After writing the foregoing letter, the distinguished legal expert got up and went into the kitchen where his wife was knitting and watching her stew. Tossing the eight above-mentioned twenty-peseta coins into her lap, he said to her in a harsh, curt tone of voice: "Here you are, Encarnación, buy more wheat, because the price is sure to go up as we approach harvest time, and don't let them gyp you on the measurement. Make my breakfast while I go to mail this letter to Seville and ask about the price of barley. I want the egg well cooked and the chocolate light, not the way I usually get them."

The attorney's wife said not a word and continued knitting like an automaton.

V

Two weeks later, on a picture-perfect day in January, the kind of day seen only in northern Africa and southern Europe, the choirmaster of the cathedral of Ceuta was sunning himself on the terrace roof of his two-story house with the peace of mind of someone who has played the organ at High Mass and then eaten a pound of anchovies, another of meat, and one of bread, while consuming an equivalent amount of wine from Tarifa.*

The good musician, as corpulent as a fattened pig and as red as a beet, was digesting with difficulty as his clouded, sluggish gaze took in the magnificent sweep of the Mediterranean, the Strait of Gibraltar and the accursed rock from which it derives its name, the nearby peaks of Anghera and Benzú, and the remote snows of the Rif Atlas,* when he heard quickened steps on the stairs and the silvery voice of his wife, who was crying delightedly: "Bonifacio! Bonifacio! A letter from Ugíjar! A letter from your uncle! And is it ever thick!"

"My, my!" exclaimed the choirmaster, turning around like a terrestrial globe or sphere on the axis where his round sel rested on the seat. "What saint do you suppose decided to make my uncle remember me? For fifteen years now I've been living in this country that was seized from Muhammad, and this, mind you, is the first time he has written to me, in spite of the fact that I've written to him dozens and dozens of times. No doubt he wants me to do something for him."

And having said this, he opened the missive (trying to keep the Pepa of the postscript from reading it), and there appeared, rustling and wanting to unroll on its own, the yellowed parchment.

"What is he sending us?" asked his wife, who was a native of Cádiz and blond into the bargain, and spirited and very attractive in spite of her forty summers.

"Pepita, don't be so inquisitive. I'll tell you, if there's a reason to tell you, as soon as I know myself. I've warned you a thousand times to respect my letters!"

"A warning typical of a rake like you! In any event, get on with it, and we'll see if I'm allowed to know the contents of this worthless piece of paper that your uncle's sending you. It looks to me like a banknote from the other world."

While his wife was saying these and other things, the musician read the letter, and it astonished him to such an extent that he got to his feet effortlessly.

But the habit of concealing his true thoughts was so ingrained in him that he managed to say in an offhand manner: "What rubbish! That evil man is clearly going senile! Would you believe that he's sent me this leaf from a bible in Hebrew so I can look for some Jew who'll buy it? And the nincompoop imagines that it'll bring him a fortune. At the same time," he added, in order to change the conversation while putting the letter and parchment in his pocket, "at the same time he asks me with considerable interest if we have children."

"He doesn't have any!" Pepita alertly observed. "No doubt he intends to name us as his heirs!"

"It's more likely that the big miser has taken it in his head to inherit *us*! But enough said, it's striking eleven and I have to tune the organ for this afternoon's vespers. I'm off. Listen, sweetheart, have dinner ready at one, and don't forget to put a few nice potatoes into the stew. Do we have children, he asks. I'm ashamed to have to tell him that we don't."

"Now listen. Hold on. It's not my fault!" the other half shot back. "You know full well that in my first marriage I had a stillborn child."

"Yes, yes! In your first marriage! As if that could be a source of satisfaction for me. One of these days you'll give me occasion to relate to you all the escapades of my bachelor days."

"Go on, you bumpkin, you tub, you ingrate! Who else in the world would have loved you like this foolish woman, who, with that potbelly and all, considers you the most handsome man God has created?"

"What? Did you say *handsome?* Well, look here, Pepa," the organist replied, thinking for sure about the Arabic parchment, "if my uncle ever does name me as his heir, or if I become rich by any other means, I swear I'll take you to live on Plaza de San Antonio in Cádiz and buy you more jewelry than Granada's Virgin of Sorrows has! So I'll see you later, my love." And pinching her already dimpled chin, he took his hat and headed toward . . . not the cathedral, but the narrow streets where Moorish families who have settled in that stronghold usually live.

VI

AT the door of a very humble but whitewashed old house in the narrowest of those streets, a man of about thirty-five or forty sat on the sill, or rather on his heels, smoking a sun-dried clay pipe. He was a Moor who peddled in his home or in the market, with a 100 percent return, the eggs and chickens brought to him at the gates of Ceuta by the independent peasants of Sierra Bullones and Sierra Bermeja. He wore a white woolen *djellabah* and a black woolen *haik*, and was called Fat Hands by the Spaniards and Admet-ben-Carime-el-Abdoun by the Moroccans.

As soon as the Moor saw the choirmaster, he rose and went to meet him, making deep salaams, and when they were face to face he said warily: "Want you little Moorish girl? I bring tomorrow nice thing, twelve years."

"My wife doesn't want any more Moorish girls," replied the musician with a rare display of dignity.

Fat Hands started to laugh.

"Besides," Don Bonifacio continued, "your diabolical little Moorish girls are very dirty."

"Wash . . ." responded the Moor, crossing his arms and tilting his head.

"I'm telling you I don't want any," repeated Don Bonifacio. "What I need today is that you, the interpreter here in the Moorish quarter because you know so much, translate this document into Spanish for me."

Fat Hands took it and with his first glimpse murmured: "It Arabic."

"Of course it's Arabic! But I want to know what it says, and if you don't pull a fast one on me I'll give you a generous gift when I settle the matter that I'm entrusting to your loyalty."

Meanwhile, Admet-ben-Carime, glancing through the entire parchment, had turned very pale.

"Do you see that it has to do with a great treasure?" the choirmaster half-affirmed, half-questioned.

"Think so," stammered the Muhammadan.

"What do you mean 'think'? Your very agitation *says* so."

"Excuse . . . ," replied Fat Hands, sweating profusely. "Are words here in modern Arabic and I understand. Are other words in old or classical Arabic and I not understand."

"What do the words that you understand say?"

"Say *gold*, say *pearls*, say *curse of Allah* but . . . I not understand meaning, explanations, marks. Need see dervish of Anghera, who is wise man, and he translate all. I take parchment today and bring tomorrow back, and not trick, not rob Señor Tudela. Moor swear!" So saying, he crossed his hands, raised them to his lips, and kissed them fervently.

Don Bonifacio thought for a moment: he recognized that in order to decipher the document he would have to rely on some Moor, and that none was as familiar or attached to him as Fat Hands, and so he agreed to leave the manuscript with him, although not without having the Moor swear repeatedly that he would return from Anghera the following day with the translation, while for his part, he, Bonifacio, swore to the Moor that he would give him at least one hundred *duros* when the treasure was discovered.

The Moslem and the Christian said goodbye to each other, and the latter headed, not for home, not for the cathedral, but for a friend's office, where he wrote the following letter:

SEÑOR DON MATÍAS DE QUESADA Y SÁNCHEZ

Alpujarra, UGÍJAR

My dearest uncle:

Thank God that we have received news of you and Aunt Encarnación, and that all is as well as Josefa and I have wished it would be. We, dear uncle, although younger than the two of you, are ailing and are weighed down with children, who will soon be orphaned and begging.

You were taken in by whomever told you that the parchment you sent me contained the key to a treasure. I had it translated by a very competent person and it turned out to be a string of blasphemies against Our Lord Jesus Christ, the Blessed Virgin and the heavenly host, written in Arabic verses by a Moorish dog from the marquisate of El Cenet, during the rebellion of Aben-Humeya. In light of such sacrilege, and on the advice of Father Confessor, I've just burned that impious testimony to Muhammadan perversity.

Remembrances to my aunt, and regards to both of you from Josefa, who is in an interesting condition for the tenth time, and please send some relief to your nephew, who is nothing but skin and bone as a result of the miserable stomach affliction.

Bonifacio

Ceuta, 29 January 1821

VII

WHILE the choirmaster was writing and mailing the preceding letter, Admet-ben-Carime-el-Abdoun was gathering together in a not too large bundle all his personal effects and possessions, which were limited to three old *haiks*, two goat's-hair cloaks, a mortar for making couscous, an iron oil lamp, and a copper pot full of pesetas (which he dug up from a corner of the little courtyard of his house). With all this, he loaded his only wife, slave, odalisque, or whatever she was— and she was uglier than a suddenly imparted piece of bad news and filthier than her husband's conscience—and departed from Ceuta, telling the watchguard at the gate that opens onto the Moorish countryside that they were going to Fez* for a change of air on the advice of the veterinarian. And inasmuch as from that time until now, a period of sixty years, no one in Ceuta or its environs has ever heard another word about Fat Hands, it goes without saying that Don Bonifacio Tudela y González did not have the pleasure of receiving from him in person the translation of the parchment—not the following day, nor the day after, nor the rest of his life, which to be sure, must have been very short, since, according to reliable information, it appears that his adored Pepita married in Marbella, for the third time, an Asturian drum major who fathered four children as pretty as a picture, and that she was widowed once again at the death of the absolute king,* at which time she secured by competitive examination in Málaga the title of midwife and the position of customs matron.

So let us follow Fat Hands and see what happened to the interesting document.

VIII

ADMET-ben-Carime-el-Abdoun breathed happily, and even did a little dance step, without losing his loose-fitting slippers, as soon as he was outside the reinforced walls of the Spanish stronghold with all of Africa before him—

because Africa, for a true African like Fat Hands, is the land of absolute freedom, of a freedom anterior to and superior to all human constitutions and institutions, of a freedom similar to that of wild rabbits and other mountain, valley, or desert animals.

Africa, I mean to say, is the earthly paradise of transgressors, the haven of impunity, the neutral ground of man and beast, protected by the heat and the expanse of the deserts. As for the sultans, kings, and beys who presume to rule in that part of the world, and the authorities and soldiers who represent them, it can be said that they amount, for their subjects, to what the hunter does for hares and stags: a possible unlucky encounter, which very few have in life, and in which he dies or does not die; if he does die, a year later the day of his death is remembered; and if he does not die, he puts the matter behind him by getting as far away as possible. Let this digression serve as a warning to whoever may need it, and let us proceed with our story.

"Zama, turn here!" the Moor said to his weary wife, as if he were talking to a beast of burden. And, instead of heading west, that is to say, toward the Anghera Gap, in search of the holy wise man or dervish, as he had indicated to Don Bonifacio, he turned south along a ravine overgrown with thickets and wild trees that presently brought him to the Tetuán road, or rather to the indistinct path which, following the contours of headlands and beaches, leads to Cape Negro by way of the valleys of Tarajar and Castillejos, Mount Negrón, and the pools of the Azmir River, names which every well-bred Spaniard will today read with love and veneration, but which at that time no one had yet heard pronounced in Spain or in the rest of the civilized world.

When ben-Carime and Zama had arrived at the little valley of Tarajar, they stopped for a rest at the edge of a brook of potable water that originates in the heights of Sierra Bullones and crosses over the valley floor; and in that safe and rugged solitude that seemed to have recently issued from the Creator's hands while remaining untouched by human ones, a vantage point that took in a solitary sea cleaved only on an occasional moonlit night by pirate skiffs or the authorized ships from Europe charged with giving them chase, the Moorish woman set about bathing and combing her hair as Fat Hands pulled out the manuscript and reread it with as much emotion as the first time.

The Arabic parchment said as follows:

May the blessing of Allah be upon all good men who read these words.

There is no other glory than the glory of Allah, of whom Muhammad was and is, in the hearts of all believers, prophet and messenger.

Men who rob the house of one who is away at war or in exile live under the curse of Allah and Muhammad, and die eaten up by beetles and cockroaches.

Blessed, then, be Allah, who raised these and other vermin in order for them to feed on evil men!

I am the kaid Hassan-ben-Jussef, slave of Allah, even though I have been wrongly called Don Rodrigo de Acuña by the successors of the Christian dogs who, by forcing them and violating solemn surrenders, baptized, using a broom for an aspergillum, my unfortunate ancestors as well as many other Islamites of these kingdoms.

I am a captain under the banner of him who, since the death of Aben-Humeya, is rightfully called king of the Andalusians, Muley-Abdalá-Mahamud-Aben-Aboó, and if he is not presently sitting on the throne of Granada it is because of the treachery and cowardice with which the Moors of Valencia have gone back on their promises and oaths, failing to rise at the same time as the Moors of Granada against the common oppressor; but they will receive their just deserts from Allah, and, if we are conquered, they too will be conquered and in the end expelled from Spain, without the merit of having fought until the last moment on the field of honor and in defense of justice, and if we are the victors we will slit their throats and throw their heads to the hogs.

I am, finally, master of the Tower and of all the land that surrounds it, as far west as the ravine of the Fox and as far east as the ravine of the Asparagus, which owes its name to the many and choice asparagus plants grown there by my grandfather, Sidi-Jussef-ben-Jussuf.

Things are not going well. Ever since the baseborn Don Juan de Austria* (May Allah confound him) came to fight against the believers, we foresee that for the present we are going to be defeated, even though over the years or even centuries another prince of the blood of the Prophet might come to regain the throne of Granada, which for seven hundred years has belonged to the Moors and will once again belong to them when Allah so wills, with the same right by which it was possessed heretofore by Vandals and Goths, and before them by the Romans, and before them by those other Africans called Carthaginians—by the right of conquest! But I repeat: I know that at present things are not going well, and that very soon I shall have to move to Morocco with my forty-three children, assuming that the Austrians do not capture me in the first battle and hang me from a cork oak, as I would hang all of them if I could.

Wherefore, upon quitting this tower in order to undertake the last and decisive campaign, I leave hidden here, in a place where no one can reach without first coming across this manuscript, all my gold, all my silver, and all my pearls; as well as my family's treasure, my parents' and my and my heirs' possessions, of which fortune I am owner and master by human and divine law, as is the bird of the feathers that it grows, or the child of the teeth that he cuts with difficulty, or every mortal of the bad humors, cancerous or leprous, that he inherits from his parents.

Stop, therefore, you Moor or Christian or Jew, who, having set out to demolish this my house, have managed to discover and read the lines that I am writing! Stop and respect your fellow man's coffer! Do not lay your hands on his fortune! Do not make off with another's possessions! There is nothing here from the national treasury, nothing from public funds, nothing from the state. The gold in mines will belong to whoever discovers it, with a portion to be given to the king of the realm. But melted and minted gold—money, coins—belongs to its owner and only to its owner. So do not rob me, you evil man! Do not rob my descendants, because they will come, on the day that it is written, to collect their inheritance. And if you readily chance upon my treasure, I advise you to publish proclamations, announcing and reporting the case to the assignees of Hassan-ben-Jussef, because honest men do not keep finds when these finds have a rightful owner.

If you do not do so, may you be damned, under Allah's curse and mine! And may a bolt of lightning cut you in two! And may every one of my coins and every one of my pearls turn into scorpions in your hands! And may your children die of leprosy, with their fingers putrefied and disintegrated so that they cannot even have the pleasure of scratching themselves! And may all the women that you love and fatten up amuse themselves and make merry with your slaves! And may your oldest daughter run off with a Jew! And you—may you be run through with a stake, hoisted on high, and exposed to public ridicule until the weight of your body pushes the stake through your crown and you end up on the ground splayed like a miserable frog impaled on a spit!

Now you know and may everyone know, and blessed be Allah who is Allah!

At the Tower of Zoraya, in Aldeire, El Cenet, the fifteenth day of the month of Safar in the year of the Hegira 968."

                                        HASSAN-BEN-JUSSEF

IX

FAT Hands was deeply troubled by his second reading of this document, not because of the moral maxims and the dreadful curses that it contained, for the scoundrel had lost his faith in Allah and Muhammad as a result of his frequent dealings with the Christians and Jews of Tetuán and Ceuta, who, naturally, laughed at the Koran, but because he believed that his face, his accent, and other Moslem features of his person prevented him from going to Spain, where he would be exposed to certain death as soon as any Christian man or woman discovered in him an enemy of the Virgin Mary.

Besides, what help (in Fat Hands's opinion) could a foreigner, a Moslem, a semibarbarian, expect from the laws or the authorities of Spain in acquiring the Tower of Zoraya to excavate it, to take possession of the treasure or to not lose it immediately along with his life?

"I have no choice!" he said to himself after reflecting for a long time. "I need to trust that renegade ben-Munuza. He's a Spaniard, and his company will deliver me from all kinds of danger in that land. But as there is no more evil man on the face of the earth than said renegade, it won't hurt for me to take a few precautions."

And in consequence of this determination, he took writing materials from his pocket, wrote a letter, put it in an envelope, which he sealed with some chewed bread, and started laughing diabolically.

Right away he looked over at his wife, who was continuing with her ablutions of an entire year at the expense of the physical and . . . moral cleanliness of the unfortunate brook, and whistling to get her attention, he deigned to speak to her as follows: "Come and sit next to me, prickle puss, and listen carefully. You can finish washing up later, because need it you do, and maybe then I'll consider you deserving of something better than the daily thrashing by which I show my affection for you. For now, you shameless thing, stop pulling faces and pay close attention to what I'm going to tell you."

The Moorish woman, who, with her hair washed and combed, looked younger and more artistic, although no less ugly than before, licked her lips like a cat, fixed on Fat Hands the two carbuncles that served her as eyes, and said to him, revealing her broad, snow-white teeth that looked like nothing human: "Speak, my lord, for your slave only wishes to serve you."

Fat Hands continued: "If at any time in the future I am the victim of some misfortune or I disappear from the world without having said goodbye to you, or having said goodbye to you, you have no news from me in six weeks, try to get back to Ceuta and mail this letter. Do you catch my meaning, monkey face?"

Zama burst into tears and exclaimed: "Admet! Do you intend to leave me?"

"Don't sound like an ass, woman!" replied the Moor. "Who's talking about that now? You know full well that you please me and are of service to me. But the question now is if you've clearly understood what I've asked you to do."

"Let me have it!" said the Moorish woman, loosening her jerkin and taking the letter, which she tucked inside her dark, heavy bosom, next to her heart. "If anything bad happens to you, this letter will be dropped in the mail at Ceuta, even though afterward I may drop in my grave."

Aben-Carime smiled in a human way upon hearing these words, and he condescended to look at his wife as if she were actually a person.

X

THAT night the Moslem couple must have fallen into a long and deep sleep among the thickets along the trail, because it was already nine o'clock the following morning when they reached the foot of Cape Negro.

At that site there was a hamlet of Arab shepherds and peasants called Medik, which consisted of a few huts, a *marabout* or Muhammadan hermitage, and a well of drinking water, with its stone curb and copper pail, like the ones depicted in some biblical scenes.

The hamlet was completely deserted at that hour. All its inhabitants had already gone off with their livestock or tools to the neighboring woods and valleys.

"Wait for me here," said Fat Hands to his wife. "I'm going to look for ben-Munuza, who ought to be on the other side of that hill over there plowing the poor soil of his land."

"Ben-Munuza!" exclaimed Zama in horror. "The renegade you've talked about!"

"Don't worry," said Fat Hands. "Today I have the upper

hand. I'll be back in a few hours and you'll see—he'll be hard on my heels like a submissive dog. This is his hut. Wait here and make us a nice meal of couscous with the corn and fat that you'll find inside. And you know that I like it cooked real well. Another thing. If you see that it's getting dark and I haven't come down, you go up; and if you don't find me on the other slope of the hill or if you find my body, return to Ceuta and mail the letter. One more thing: assuming that it's my body that you find, search me to see if ben-Munuza has stolen the parchment. If he has stolen it, go from Ceuta to Tetuán and report the murder and robbery to the authorities. That covers everything. Goodbye."

The Moorish woman cried her eyes out as Fat Hands set off on the path that led to the top of the nearby hill.

XI

ONCE over the top, Fat Hands soon spotted in the next valley a burly Moor dressed in white, who, after the manner of a patriarch, was plowing the black earth with the aid of a magnificent yoke of oxen. The man looked like a statue of Peace sculpted in marble. But he was none other than the sullen and dreaded renegade ben-Munuza, whose story will horrify readers when they learn the truth of it.

For the present, be content to know that he was about forty years old, that he was crude, tough, agile, and had a gloomy expression, even though his eyes were as blue as the sky and his beard as golden as the African sun that had bronzed the white European face with which he had been born.

"Good morning, Fat Hands!" shouted in Castilian the one-time Spaniard as soon as he spied the Moroccan. And his voice expressed the melancholy joy typical of the foreigner who has occasion to speak his native tongue.

"Good morning, Juan Falgueira!" ben-Carime responded sarcastically.

Upon hearing such a greeting, the renegade shook from head to toe and grasped the iron share of the plow as if to defend himself. "What name did you just use?" he asked, moving toward Fat Hands.

The latter, who was laughing, waited for him and answered in Arabic, with a courage of which no one would have believed him capable: "I used . . . your real name—the name you had in Spain when you were a Christian, which I've known since I was in Oran* three years ago."

"In Oran?"

"Yes, sir. In Oran. What's so extraordinary about that? You had come to Morocco from there, which was where I had gone to buy hens. I described you and inquired about your background, which several Spaniards related to me. So I found out that you were a Galician, that your name was Juan Falgueira, and that you had escaped from the maximum security prison in Granada, where you were awaiting execution for having robbed and killed, fifteen years ago, some men for whom you worked as a muleteer. Can you doubt that I know about you like the back of my hand?"

"Tell me, my friend," replied the renegade in a still voice as he glanced around, "have you told this story to any Moroccans? Does anyone in this damned land know about it besides you? Because the fact is that I want to live in peace, without having anyone or anything reminding me of that fateful act for which I've paid dearly. I'm poor; I have no family, no country, no language; not even the God who created me. I live among enemies, with no other assets than these oxen and these parcels of barren land, which I bought with ten years of the sweat of my brow. So you've made a big mistake by coming here and telling me—"

"Wait!" a very alarmed Fat Hands interrupted him. "Don't give me those fierce looks—I've come to do you a huge favor, not provoke you for the fun of it. I haven't mentioned your unfortunate story to a soul. What for? Every secret might be a treasure, and he who tells it loses it. But there are times when an exchange of secrets can be highly useful. Like, for instance, right now: I'm going to tell you an important secret of mine, which will serve as security for yours, and which will oblige us to be lifelong friends."

"I'm listening. Go on," the renegade calmly responded.

Aben-Carime then read to him the Arabic parchment, which Juan Falgueira listened to without batting an eye, and as if he were angry, which the Moor noticed; and so as to fully gain his trust, Fat Hands also disclosed to him that he had stolen that document from a Christian in Ceuta.

The Spaniard smiled slightly when he realized that the egg and hen peddler must have feared him a great deal to reveal that theft when there was no need. For his part, Fat Hands, encouraged by ben-Munuza's smile, finally got down to brass tacks, speaking as follows: "I assume that you have grasped the importance of this document and the reason I've read it to you. I don't know where the Tower of Zoraya is, or Aldeire, or El Cenet; I wouldn't know how to get *to* Spain, nor how to get around *in* Spain. Furthermore, they would kill me there for not being a Christian, or at the very least they would steal the treasure from me, either before or after I discovered it. For all these reasons I need to be accompanied by a trustworthy, reliable Spaniard, of whose life I shall be master and whom I can have hanged with a single word, a Spaniard, in short, like you, Juan Falgueira, who, after all, has not profited at all by robbing and killing. Look at you. You work like a horse, when with the millions that I'm going to give you, you can go off to America or to France or to India to enjoy yourself and live it up, and maybe even become a king. What do you think of my scheme?"

"That it's well hatched, like the work of a Moor," replied ben-Munuza, in whose strong hands, crossed behind his back, the iron bar dangled to and fro like a tiger's tail.

Fat Hands smiled smugly, thinking that his proposition had been accepted.

"Nevertheless," the gloomy Galician then added, "you have failed to take into account one thing."

"What?" ben-Carime inquired comically, tilting his head back and not looking anywhere in particular, like someone who is getting ready to listen to nonsense and silliness.

"You have failed to take into account that I would be a jackass if I were to go back to Spain with you to put you in possession of . . . half a treasure, relying on you to put me in possession of the other half! I say so because you would only have to speak one word on the day that we arrived at Aldeire, when you believed yourself free from danger, and you could slip away from me and wriggle out of giving me half of the treasure. To tell the truth, you're not nearly as clever as you think you are, just a poor devil worthy of pity who's come to a dead end by revealing to me the location of that great treasure and telling me at the same time that you know my history, and that if I were to go to Spain with you, you would be the absolute master of my life! Well . . . what do I need you for? Why do I need your help to go and seize the entire treasure? Why do I need you in the world? Who are you, now that you've read the parchment to me, now that I can take it away from you?"

"What are you saying?" shrieked Fat Hands, suddenly feeling the coldness of death penetrate his bones.

"I'm not saying anything. . . . Take that!" replied Juan Falgueira, striking a terrible blow with the iron bar on the head of ben-Carime, who toppled to the ground, blood issuing from his eyes, nose, and mouth, unable to utter a word.

The poor devil was dead.

XII

THREE or four weeks after Fat Hands's death, around the 20th of February, 1821, it was snowing like all get-out in the town of Aldeire, and all throughout the magnificent Andalusian sierra, which takes its existence and name from the snow.*

It was Shrove Sunday, and the church bell, with its thin, pure sound like the voice of a child, was summoning to Mass for the fourth time the frozen faithful of that parish that found itself too close to heaven, Christians who could not bring themselves, on a such a raw, bleak day, to leave their beds or the warmth of a fire, claiming perhaps, as a pretext, that "during Shrovetide one shouldn't worship God but the devil."

Something of the sort at least was being said by Uncle Juan Gómez to his pious wife, Señá Torcuata, as he

defended himself in the corner by the fire against the arguments with which she begged him not to drink any more
brandy or eat any more doughnuts and instead accompany
her to Mass, like a good Christian, unafraid of the criticisms
of the schoolteacher and other liberal voters. But at the
height of the heated discussion, Uncle Jenaro, His Honor's
head shepherd, turned up in the kitchen, and, taking off his
hat and scratching his head all at once, said: "May God give
us a good day, Señor Juan and Señá Torcuata! I expect you
understand that something has happened up there for me to
come down in this awful weather when it's not my Sunday to
hear Mass. Are both of you in good health?"

"Well, I'm not waiting any longer!" exclaimed the mayor's
wife, throwing on her mantilla furiously. "It must be God's
will that you not hear Mass today! You have enough conversation and brandy here for the whole day, so carry on about
whether the goats are with young or whether the lambs have
sprouted horns. You'll lose your soul, Juan, you'll lose your
soul if you don't soon make your peace with the Church by
giving up that accursed mayoralty."

When Señá Torcuata had gone, the mayor handed a
doughnut and a glass of brandy to his head shepherd and
said: "Women's foolishness, Uncle Jenaro. Pull up to the fire
and tell me the news. What's going on up there?"

"Wait till you hear! Yesterday afternoon, Francisco, the
goatherd, saw that a man dressed like a native of Málaga—in
long pants, a linen jacket, and wrapped in a travel blanket—
had gone into the new corral through the section that's not
walled in yet, and that he was walking around the Moor's
Tower, studying it and measuring it as if he were a master
builder. Francisco asked him what he was doing, and the
stranger in turn asked who the owner of the tower was, and
when Francisco replied that it was none other than the
mayor of the town, the man said that he would speak to His
Honor in the evening and explain his plans to him. Night fell
quickly, and it looked as though the man was leaving, so the
goatherd shut himself up in his hut, which, as you know, is
not far from there. Two hours later, after it had gotten
completely dark, the same Francisco heard some very

strange noises coming from the tower and saw that a light was burning there, all of which threw such a scare into him that he didn't dare to go to my hut to inform me. He waited until daybreak, when he recounted to me yesterday afternoon's incident, as well as the fact that those noises in the tower lasted all night. Since I'm an old man and have served the king and am not frightened by many things, I immediately headed for the Moor's Tower, accompanied by a trembling Francisco, and we found the stranger wrapped in his blanket and sleeping in a poky little room on the ground floor that still has its concrete dome. I awakened the suspicious stranger and upbraided him for having spent the night in another person's house without the owner's permission, to which he answered that the tower wasn't a house, just a pile of rubble where a poor traveler could rightly seek shelter on a snowy night, and that he was prepared to come before you and explain who he was and the undertakings and ideas that he had in mind. So I brought him with me and he's out in the yard with the goatherd, waiting for you to give him permission to come in."

"Let him come in!" said Uncle Ant, standing up, very perturbed because it had occurred to him as soon as the head shepherd began to speak that the stranger and his actions went hand in hand with the celebrated treasure, the discovery of which, through his own efforts, had stymied His Honor a week before, when he had torn out in vain numerous and very heavy foundation stones.

XIII

Now we have, face to face and alone, Uncle Juan Gómez and the stranger.

"What's your name?" the former asked the latter with all the haughtiness of a small town mayor and without inviting him to sit down.

"My name is Jaime Olot," the mysterious man replied.

"Your accent doesn't sound like a native one. Are you English?"

"I'm Catalan."

"Well, well. Catalan. That's fine. So . . . what brings you here? Above all, why the devil were you taking measurements at my tower yesterday?"

"I'll tell you. I'm a miner by profession and I've come to look for work in these parts, which are famous for their copper and silver mines. Yesterday afternoon, as I was passing by the Moor's Tower, I saw that a wall was being built with stones that had been removed from it, but that it would still be necessary to knock down or tear out numerous others in order to complete the wall. Demolition is right up my alley, either with explosive charges or with my bare hands, because I'm as strong as an ox, and it occurred to me that I might arrange a contract to raze it completely and dig up the foundations, assuming that I could come to an agreement with the owner."

Uncle Ant winked his little gray eyes and slyly responded: "Well, sir, I'm not interested in such a contract."

"Understand that I'll do all the work for very little money, almost for nothing."

"Now I'm even less interested!"

The so-called Jaime Olot considered the equivocal response given by Uncle Juan Gómez and stared hard at him, trying to fathom the meaning of such a reply, but, failing to read anything in His Honor's foxlike countenance, it seemed to him like an opportune moment to add, with feigned naturalness: "I wouldn't be unhappy either about repairing a section of that old building and living in it, tilling the land that you intend to use for a corral. So I'll buy them both from you—the Moor's Tower and the land that surrounds it!"

"I'm not interested in selling it," responded Uncle Ant.

"I'm prepared to pay you twice as much as it's worth!" answered emphatically the self-styled Catalan.

"For that reason I'm even less interested!" repeated the Andalusian with such insulting sarcasm that his interlocutor took a step back, like someone who realizes he's skating on thin ice.

So Jaime Olot reflected for a moment and then, raising his

head in a resolute manner and putting his hands behind his back, he said through cynical laughter: "Then you know that there's a treasure on that ground!"

Uncle Juan Gómez leaned forward, because he was seated, and, looking at the Catalan from head to toe, exclaimed very wittily: "What startles me is that you know it!"

"Well, it would startle you even more if I told you that I'm the only one who knows it for certain."

"In other words you know the exact spot where the treasure is buried?"

"I know the exact spot, and in less than twenty-four hours I could unearth all the riches that sleep there in the shade."

"That means. . . . Do you possess a certain document?"

"Yes, sir. I have a parchment that dates back to the time of the Moors, a half yard square, in which everything is explained."

"Tell me . . . and that document?"

"I'm not carrying it on my person, nor is there reason to do so, as I know it by heart, word for word, in Spanish and Arabic. Oh, I'm not so stupid as to give myself up bag and baggage! Which means that before coming to these parts I hid the parchment where no one can find it except me."

"Well, then, there's no more to be said. Señor Jaime Olot, let's be straightforward with each other like two good friends," the mayor proposed, pouring the stranger a glass of brandy.

"Let's!" agreed the stranger, taking a seat without leave and downing his drink.

"Tell me," continued Uncle Ant, "and tell me without lying so that I can begin to take you at your word."

"Ask away, but I'll remain silent when it's in my interest to keep something back."

"Do you come from Madrid?"

"No, sir. I was in the capital twenty-five years ago, but that was the first and last time."

"Do you come from the Holy Land?"

"No, sir. I'm not so inclined."

"Do you know a lawyer from Ugíjar named Don Matías de Quesada?"

"No, sir. I detest lawyers and all masters of the pen."

"Well, then, how did that parchment pass into your possession?"

Jaime Olot remained silent.

"That I like! I see that you don't want to lie!" exclaimed the mayor. "But it's also true that Don Matías de Quesada took me for a ride, robbing me of two ounces of gold and then selling that document to someone in Melilla or Ceuta. And another thing: although you're not a Moor, you look as though you've lived among Moors."

"Don't waste your breath or your time. I'll clear up your doubts. That lawyer must have sent the manuscript to a Spaniard in Ceuta, from whom it was stolen three weeks ago by the Moor who passed it on to me."

"Of course! Now I get it! He probably sent it to a nephew of his who's a musician at the cathedral there. Bonifacio de Tudela, I think is his name."

"That could be."

"What a cheat that Don Matías is! To swindle his *compadre* like that! But look how chance has brought the parchment back to my hands!"

"You mean to mine," observed the stranger.

"To ours!" replied the mayor, pouring more brandy. "Well, sir, we're millionaires! We'll divide the treasure half and half, considering that you can't dig in that ground without my permission and that I can't find the treasure without the help of the parchment that has become yours. In other words, fate has made us brothers. From this day forward you'll live in my house! Let's have another glass! And once we finish breakfast, we'll start our excavations."

At this point Señá Torcuata returned from Mass, and her husband, after introducing Jaime Olot, related to her what they had been discussing. The good woman heard with equal parts of fear and joy that the treasure was about to turn up; she repeatedly made the sign of the cross while listening to the betrayal and villainy of their *compadre* Don Matías de Quesada, and looked with dread at the stranger whose physiognomy caused her to have terrible forebodings of great misfortune.

Realizing, then, that she had to feed that man breakfast, she went into her larder to gather the most essential and select items from her stores—in other words, pickled loins and pork sausages from the last slaughter, not without saying to herself as she took the lids off the jars: "It's about time that treasure turned up, because, what with discovery or no discovery, it's already cost us thirty-two *duros* for the famous cup of chocolate, the longtime friendship of our *compadre* Don Matías, these beautiful slices that would have been so delicious with peppers and tomatoes in August, and having as a guest a mean-looking stranger. May there be a curse on treasures, and mines, and devils, and everything underground except water and the faithful departed."

XIV

THESE thoughts were crossing Señá Torcuata's mind and she was already heading toward the fireplace, a skillet in each hand, when a hubbub rose in the street, the yelling and whistling of old women and children, along with the voices of graver people who were shouting: "Mister Mayor! Open the door! The city authorities are entering the town with troops of soldiers!"

Jaime Olot turned green around the gills upon hearing those words and, wringing his hands, he said: "Hide me, Mister Mayor! Otherwise we'll have no treasure! The authorities are coming in search of *me*!"

"In search of *you?* For what reason? Are you some kind of criminal?"

"I was right!" cried Aunt Torcuata. "Nothing good could come from that cheerless face. All this is Lucifer's doing!"

"Quickly! Quickly!" the stranger added. "Take me out through the yard gate!"

"All right, but first tell me where to find the treasure," replied Uncle Ant.

"Mister Mayor!" the people at the door kept calling. "Open up! The town is surrounded! It seems that the man you've been talking to for a half hour is wanted!"

"Open up to the authorities of the lower court!" shouted finally an imperious voice that was accompanied by loud knocks on the door.

"There's nothing we can do!" said the mayor, going to open up while the stranger made for the back door to leave by the yard.

But the head shepherd and the goatherd, who were on the lookout, blocked his way, and between them and the soldiers, who were also coming in through that door, they caught him and tied him up without mishap, although that devil of a man displayed the strength and agility of a tiger in the struggle.

The bailiff of the court, under whose orders were one clerk and twenty infantrymen, was in the meantime relating to the terrified mayor the causes and grounds for that spectacular arrest. "That man," he was saying, "with whom you've been shut up, I don't know why, talking about I don't know what, is the famous Galician, Juan Falgueira, who fifteen years ago, in a house on the plains of Granada, robbed and slit the throats of several men for whom he was working as a muleteer. He escaped from the chapel the day before his execution, dressed in the habit of the monk who was ministering to him, whom he left nearly strangled to death. The king himself, whom God save, received a letter from Ceuta two weeks ago signed by a Moor named Fat Hands, saying that Juan Falgueira, after having lived for a long time in Oran and other parts of Africa, was going to set sail for Spain, and that it would be easy to capture him in Aldeire, El Cenet, where he intended to buy a Moorish tower and devote himself to mining. At the same time, the Spanish consul in Tetuán wrote to the government here, declaring that a Moorish woman named Zama had come before him to protest that the Spanish renegade Ben-Munuza, formerly Juan Falgueira, had just set sail for Spain after murdering the Moor Fat Hands, husband of the complainant, and having robbed him of a certain valuable parchment. For all of which, and most especially for the attempt on the monk's life in the chapel, His Majesty the king has recommended to the Court of Justice of Granada, in the strongest of terms, the apprehension of said criminal and his immediate execution in the same city of Granada."

The reader can well imagine the terror and astonishment of all the people who heard this account, as well as the anguish of Uncle Ant, for whom there could no longer be any doubt that the parchment was in the possession of that man sentenced to death!

So the greedy mayor, even at the risk of compromising himself more than he had already done, dared to call Juan Falgueira aside and whisper to him, after first announcing to all those present that he was going to try to persuade the criminal to confess his crimes to God and man. But what both "partners" really discussed was the following:

"My friend!" said Uncle Ant. "Not even Christian forgiveness will save you now! And surely you recognize that it would be a shame for the parchment to get lost. Tell me where you've hidden it!"

"My friend!" responded the Galician. "With that parchment, that is to say, with the treasure that it represents, I intend to negotiate my reprieve. Obtain for me the royal pardon and I'll hand over the document to you; but, for the present, I'll offer it to the judges to have them declare that in these fifteen years of expatriation the statue of limitations has run out on my crime."

"My friend!" exclaimed Uncle Ant. "You're a wise man and I'll be pleased if all your plans work out. But, if they fall through, for God's sake I ask you not to take to your grave a secret that will be of use to no one."

"You bet I'll take it with me!" replied Juan Falgueira. "I have to take revenge on the world somehow!"

"Let's get moving!" shouted the bailiff at this point, putting en end to that curious colloquy.

And the court clerks and soldiers removed the condemned man, now handcuffed and shackled, and they all left in the direction of the city of Guadix, from which point the Galician was to be transported to Granada.

"The devil! The devil!" the wife of Uncle Juan Gómez kept saying an hour later, when she returned the loin and pork sausage to their respective jars. "May there be a curse on all treasures, present and future!"

XV

NEEDLESS to say, Uncle Ant did not find a way to obtain a pardon for Juan Falgueira, nor did the judges condescend to listen seriously to the latter's offers of a treasure if they granted a stay of execution, nor did the terrible Galician agree to disclose the whereabouts of the parchment or the location of the treasure to the undaunted mayor of Aldeire, who, with that in mind, still had the stomach for visiting him in the chapel of the maximum security prison of Granada.

And so Juan Falgueira was hanged the Friday of Passion Week on the Paseo del Triunfo; and Uncle Ant, upon his return to Aldeire on Palm Sunday, fell ill with a case of typhoid fever that worsened so rapidly that on Wednesday of Holy Week he made his confession and his will, and passed away Holy Saturday morning.

But before dying he had a letter sent to Don Matías de Quesada, reproaching him for his betrayal and theft (which had caused three men to lose their lives) and forgiving him like a good Christian, on condition that he return to Señá Torcuata the thirty-two *duros* for the cup of chocolate.

This formidable letter arrived in Ugíjar at the same time as the news of Uncle Juan Gómez's death, and together they affected the old lawyer to such a degree that he never recovered, and he died shortly thereafter, although not before having written at the eleventh hour a terrible letter of his own, full of insults and curses, to his nephew, accusing the choirmaster of the cathedral of Ceuta of having deceived and robbed him and of being the cause of his death.

It is said that reading such a justified and frightful accusation precipitated the stroke that took Don Bonifacio to his grave.

So the mere suspicion of a treasure caused five deaths and other misfortunes, and in the end things remained as obscure and hidden as they had been in the beginning, inasmuch as Señá Torcuata, the only person in the world who knew the history of the storied parchment, took care never to mention it again for the rest of her life, as she considered that all of it had been the work of the devil and the necessary consequence of her husband's dealings with the enemies of the Altar and the Throne.

Well might the reader ask: How is it that we, knowing that the treasure lies hidden there, have not gone to dig it up and take possession of it? And our answer is that the highly curious story of the discovery and use of those riches, subsequent to Señá Torcuata's death, is also perfectly well known to us, and that we may tell it one day, if news reaches us that the public is interested in reading it.

The Tall Woman

A TALE OF FEAR

I

"WHAT do we know, my friends? What do we know?" asked Gabriel, a distinguished forester, sitting down under a pine tree near a fountain at the top of the Guadarrama Mountains, four and a half miles from El Escorial, on the boundary line between the provinces of Madrid and Segovia. I'm well acquainted with the fountain and the pine and can picture them easily, but I've forgotten the name of the spot. "Let's sit down, as it's de rigueur and one of the things we had planned to do," continued Gabriel. "We can rest and eat in this pleasant and traditional setting, which is famous for the digestive properties of the waters of this spring, and also for the many festive meals enjoyed here by our illustrious masters Don Miguel Bosch, Don Máximo Laguna, Don Agustín Pascual,* and other great naturalists. Then I'll tell you a strange and unusual tale as proof of my thesis, which amounts to demonstrating, even though you may call me an obstructionist, that supernatural things still occur in the world, I mean things that do not fall within the bounds of reason, science, or philosophy, as such 'words, words, words,' to quote Hamlet, are or are not understood nowadays."

153

Gabriel was making this colorful speech to five companions of various ages, none of whom was young and only one of whom was elderly. Three of them were also foresters, the fourth was a painter, the fifth was somewhat of a writer, and all had made the climb with the orator, who was the youngest, on hired donkeys from the royal residence of San Lorenzo* to spend the day gathering plants in the pine groves of Peguerinos,* catching butterflies with nets, collecting rare beetles from under the bark of rotting pines, and eating a repast of cold cuts, which they had all chipped in to buy.

The year was 1875, in the hottest part of summer. I don't remember if it was the feast of Saint James or the feast of Saint Louis*; I'm inclined to say it was that of the latter. Whichever day it was, up on that mountain top one enjoyed delightful fresh air, and everything—heart, stomach, intelligence—worked better there than out in the social world and ordinary life.

When the six friends had sat down, Gabriel continued speaking as follows: "I don't think you'll accuse me of being a visionary. Fortunately or unfortunately for me, I am, let's put it this way, a modern man, not at all superstitious, and as positivist as they come, even though I may include among the positive facts all the faculties and emotions of my spirit in matters of feeling. So then, with regard to extranatural or supernatural phenomena, listen to what I listened to and see what I saw, although I wasn't the real hero of the bizarre tale that I'm going to relate, and tell me straight off what natural, physical, factual explanation—or however we want to phrase it—can be given to such a marvelous occurrence.

"The story goes like this, but . . . first let's have a swallow or two, as the wineskin must have cooled by now in that bubbly, crystalline spring that God saw fit to place on this piney mountain top to chill the wine of botanists!"

II

"LET'S see now. I don't know if you've heard of a civil engineer named Telesforo X, who died in 1860—"

"I haven't."

"I have."

"I have too. An Andalusian with a black mustache, who was engaged to be married to the daughter of the Marquis of Moreda, but died of hepatitis and—"

"The very same," continued Gabriel. "Well, a half year before his death, my friend Telesforo was still a young man with brilliant prospects, as we say now. Handsome, strong, spirited, with the distinction of having graduated first in his class at the School of Civil Engineering, and already highly esteemed in the profession for his remarkable accomplishments, he was sought after by a number of firms in those golden years of public works,* and he was sought after as well by marriageable or unhappily married women, and of course by unrepentant widows, one of whom was a very attractive sort who. . . . But the widow in question is beside the point, since the one that Telesforo loved in earnest was his fiancée, poor Joaquinita Moreda, whereas the other involvement did not go beyond a purely 'usufructory' affair that—"

"Don Gabriel! No unseemly digressions!"

"You're right, no unseemly digressions, because neither my story nor the pending controversy lend themselves to jokes or witticisms. Juan, pour me another half glass. This is really good wine! All right, pay attention and be serious because now the sad part begins.

"As those of you who knew her are probably aware, Joaquina died suddenly at the Santa Águeda spa at the end of summer of 1859. I was in Pau when I heard the sad news, which affected me deeply because of my close friendship with Telesforo. I had spoken to her only once, at the home of her aunt, General López's widow, and of course that bluish pallor of hers, typical of people with an aneurysm, struck me right away as an indication of poor health. But, in any case, the girl stood out for her elegance, beauty, and grace, and since she was in addition an only child of a titled family, which meant that she would inherit millions, I realized that my good mathematician would be inconsolable. Consequently, as soon as I returned to Madrid, which was two or three weeks after his misfortune, I went to see him very early one morning. He had a smart bachelor apartment that doubled as his office, of which he was the manager, on Calle del Lobo.* I don't remember the number, just that it was close to the Carrera de San Jéronimo.

"Looking deeply pained and grave, but seemingly in control of his grief, the young engineer was already working at that hour with his assistants on some railroad project or other, and dressed in strict mourning. He embraced me tightly and for a long time did not utter even the slightest sigh. Then he gave instructions about the work in hand to one of those assistants and led me to his private study, located at the opposite end of the apartment, telling me along the way, mournfully and without looking at me: 'I'm very glad you've come. I've missed you and needed you. Something very strange and peculiar is happening to me, and only a friend like you could listen to my story without considering me silly or mad. I need to hear a calm, objective opinion, a scientific response.

"'Sit down,' he continued saying when we entered his study, 'and don't be afraid that I'm going to burden you by describing the grief that's tormenting me, grief that will last a lifetime. To what end? You'll be able to imagine it easily, for as little as you may understand of human sorrow, and besides, I don't wish to be consoled now, nor afterwards, nor ever. What I'm going to talk to you about in the detail that the case requires, and by that I mean starting at the very beginning, is a mysterious, horrible set of circumstances that have acted as an infernal omen to this misfortune, and which have my spirit troubled to such an extent that it'll frighten you.'

"'Tell me!' I responded, beginning to feel in fact a vague sense of regret at having entered that house, when I saw the expression of cowardice that clouded my friend's face.

"'Listen, then,' he said, mopping the sweat from his brow.

III

"'I don't know if it's because of the innate fatalism of my imagination or because of the apprehension ingrained in me while listening to some of those old wives' tales that are so unwisely used to frighten children at a tender age, but the fact is that ever since I was a tot, nothing has caused me as much horror and fright, whether I see one in my mind's eye or in reality, as a woman on the street in the small hours.

"'You know that I've never been a coward. I fought a duel, as any self-respecting man would, when it was necessary to do so, and shortly after graduating from engineering school I battled my striking workers in Despeñaperros* with a club and a gun until I brought them to heel. All my life, in Jaen,* Madrid, and other places, I've walked the streets late at night, alone and unarmed, watchful only of the amorous pursuit that kept me up, and if by chance I ran into shady-looking types, whether thieves or simple bullies, they were the ones who stepped aside or ran off, leaving the way clear for me. But if the type or shape was a woman alone, standing or walking, and if I too was alone, and not another living soul was to be seen anywhere, then—laugh if you have a mind to, but believe me—I would get goose bumps; vague fears would assault my spirit; I would think about souls in the hereafter, about fantastic beings, about the superstitious beliefs that might make me laugh in any other circumstances; and I would quicken my step or turn back, unable to shake my dread, unable to relax even for a moment until I found myself inside of my own home.

"'Once there, I would also start to laugh at myself and be ashamed of my madness, my only consolation being that no one knew of it. Then I would come to the cold realization that, as I believed neither in ghosts nor in witches nor in phantoms, I should not have feared anything from a skinny woman whom destitution, vice, or some unfortunate accident might have drawn from her home, and to whom I ought to have extended a helping hand in case she needed it, or given her alms, if she asked. Notwithstanding such a realization, this deplorable scene would be repeated over and over, and let's remember that I was twenty-five and that I had spent many of those years as a nocturnal adventurer, and never once had I found myself in a tight situation with all those solitary women who were up as late as I was. But in the end none of what I've just said ever took on any importance, because that irrational terror would vanish as soon as I arrived at my home or saw other people in the street, and minutes later I didn't even remember it, as we don't remember inconsequential, insignificant mistakes or nonsense.

"'And this is where things stood when one night almost three years ago—unfortunately I have several reasons to recall the exact date, 15 November 1857—I was returning at three o'clock in the morning, which means it was really the 16th of November, to the little place on Calle de Jardines, near Calle de la Montera, where I lived back then. The weather was miserable—windy and cold—and at that late hour I had just left . . . not a love nest, but, and I'll tell you this even though it may come as a surprise, a kind of gaming house, not known as such by the police,* but where a lot of people had already lost their shirts, and where I had been taken that night by a false friend, in the belief that all we would do was strike up an acquaintance with certain elegant ladies of doubtful virtue—pure *demimondes*—under pretext of betting a few *maravedises* at cards, played at a round table with a baize cover. And then around midnight other people arrived, from the Royal Theater and the truly aristocratic salons, and the game changed, and out came gold coins, afterward bills, and then promissory notes written in pencil. Little by little I descended into the obscure jungle of vice, which was full of fevers and temptations, and lost all that I had, and all that I possessed, and even ended up owing a fortune on an IOU. By that I mean that I was completely ruined, and that without my inheritance and the lucrative business deals that I made immediately thereafter, I would have been in a very difficult and precarious position.

"'Anyhow, as I started to say, I was returning to my house late that night, numb with cold, hungry, and ashamed and disgusted, as you can well imagine, and thinking, more than about myself, about my elderly and ailing father, to whom would have to write asking for money, which could not help but distress as well as surprise him, since he thought I had more than a comfortable salary, when, shortly after starting down my street at the end that intersects Calle de Peligros, I noticed, standing in the closed doorway of a newly built house on the side where I was walking, a very tall, strong-looking woman, as still and stiff as a wood pole, roughly sixty years of age, whose evil and bold and lashless eyes fixed on mine like two daggers, while her toothless mouth, in an attempt to smile, made a horrible face at me.

"'The very terror or delirious fear that gripped me instantaneously gave me a certain marvelous perception to distinguish in a flash, in other words, in the two seconds or so that I locked eyes with that repugnant vision, the smallest details of her figure and her dress. I'm going to see if I can convey my impressions in the manner and form that I received them, the way they were forever stamped on my mind by the light of the street lamp that illuminated such an ominous scene with a hellish gleam.

"'But I'm getting too excited, although not without cause, as you'll see further on. Nevertheless, don't worry about the state of my mind. I'm not mad yet!

"'The first thing that startled me in what I'll call that *woman* was her extreme height and the width of her scrawny shoulders; next, the roundness and the unwavering stare of her withered, owlish eyes; then, the hugeness of her prominent nose and the big middle gap in her teeth, which turned her mouth into a kind of dark hole; and, finally, her dress, like the working girls from Avapiés, the cotton kerchief around her head that was knotted under her chin, and the tiny, open fan in one hand with which she covered, affecting modesty, the middle of her bosom.

"'Nothing could have been more ridiculous and horrid, nor more absurd and sarcastic, than that minuscule fan in such enormous hands, serving as a sort of scepter of weakness for that bony, hideous, old giant of a woman! A similar effect was produced by the big, gaudy kerchief that framed her face, compared with the masculine, hawklike, molelike nose that for a moment made me wonder, not without rejoicing, if it wasn't a man in disguise. But the cynical stare and sickening smile were those of an old woman, a witch, a sorceress, a *Parca*,* something that fully justified the aversion and dread that I had been made to feel all my life by women who walked the streets alone at night. You could say that I had had, from a very early age, a premonition of that encounter. You could say that I instinctively feared it, as every living creature fears and senses and detects and recognizes his natural enemy before having suffered a single offense from him, before having seen him, merely by hearing his footsteps.

"'I didn't break into a run as soon as I saw that sphinx of my life, less from shame or manly honor than from fear that my very dread might reveal to her who I was, or that I might give her wings to pursue me, to attack me, to . . . to do I don't know what! The dangers conjured up by panic have no translatable form or name!

"'My house was at the opposite end of the long, narrow street on which I found myself alone, all alone, with that mysterious apparition whom I thought capable of annihilating me with one word. What was I gong to do to reach it? Oh! With what longing I saw in the distance the broad and well-lighted Calle de la Montera, where policemen patrol around the clock.

"'So I decided to pluck up my courage, to disguise and conceal that miserable terror, and not to quicken my step, but to continue to move steadily, even at the cost of years of life and health, and in this way little by little approach my house, trying very hard not to fall flat on my face first.

"'And that's how I walked, and I must have taken at least twenty steps beyond the doorway where the woman with the fan was hidden, when all of a sudden a horrible, terrifying, yet very rational, idea occurred to me: the idea of turning around to see if my enemy was following me!

""'It's either one thing or the other," I thought with the speed of lightning. "Either there are grounds for my terror, or it's madness. If there are grounds, that woman is probably on my heels and will overtake me, and there's no place I can turn for help. And if it's madness, apprehension, a fit of panic like any other, then I'll convince myself of that, in the present instance and for all the others to come, upon seeing that the poor old woman has stayed put in that doorway, seeking shelter from the cold or waiting for the door to be opened for her, and if such is the case, I'll be able to continue on my way very calmly, cured of a mania that is driving me to distraction."

"'Having reasoned in this manner, I made an extraordinary effort and turned around.

"'Ah, Gabriel, Gabriel! What bad fortune! The tall woman had followed me with stealthy footsteps! She was on top of me, practically touching me with her fan, practically leaning her head on my shoulder!

"'Why? For what reason, my friend? Was she a thief? Was she really a man in disguise? Was she an ironical old woman who had understood that I was afraid of her? Was she the specter of my cowardice? Was she the mocking ghost of human disappointments and shortcomings?

"'There would be no end to my telling you all the things that crossed my mind at that moment. What I did was scream and run away like a four-year-old child who thinks he's seen the bogeyman, and I didn't stop running until I came out on Calle de la Montera.

"'Once there, my fear disappeared as if by magic. In spite of the fact that Calle de la Montera was also deserted! So I turned my head back toward Calle de Jardines, which ran straight its entire length and was sufficiently well-lighted by its three street lamps and a reflection from Calle de Peligros that I couldn't lose the tall woman in the darkness in the event she had retreated in that direction, and—heaven be praised!—I didn't see her standing, walking, or in any other position.

"'Still, I refrained from reentering my street.

"'"That hag," I said to myself, "must have gone into some other doorway! But while the lamps continue to be lit, she can't move without my noticing it from here."

"'At that point I saw a night watchman appear on Calle de Caballero de Gracia, and I called out to him without moving from where I stood. I told him, to justify my call and to excite his interest, that on Calle de Jardines there was a man dressed as a woman, and that he needed to enter it by way of Calle de Peligros, which he should approach through Calle de la Aduana. I said that I would wait at that other end, and that this way the person who was unquestionably a thief or a murderer couldn't escape us.

"The night watchman did what I suggested and started down Calle de la Aduana, and then when I saw his lantern coming up Calle de Jardines, I resolutely entered it from my end.

"We soon met halfway and neither one of us had come across a soul, in spite of having searched every doorway.

"'He's probably gone into some house,' said the night watchman.

"'That must be it,' I replied, opening the door of mine with the firm determination of moving to another street the following day.

"'A few moments later I was inside of my fourth-floor apartment, having let myself in with the latchkey I always carried so as not to disturb my faithful servant José.

"'Nevertheless, that night he was waiting up for me. My misfortunes of the 15th and 16th of November had not ended!

"'What's going on?' I asked in surprise.

"'Major Falcón,' he replied, visibly moved, 'waited here for you from eleven until two-thirty, and told me that if you came home to sleep you shouldn't get dressed, because he would come back at daybreak.'

"'José's words filled me with grief and dismay, as though I had been notified of my own death. That winter, my beloved father, who lived in Jaen, had been suffering frequent and very dangerous attacks of his chronic illness, and, knowing this, I had written to my brothers that, in case of a sudden, tragic turn for the worse, they should telegraph Major Falcón, who would then get in touch with me. So I had no doubt that my father had passed away!

"'I sat down in an armchair to wait for daybreak and my friend's arrival, which would bring me official word of that crushing blow, and only God knows how much I suffered in those two hours of cruel expectation, during which—and this is what relates to the present story—I couldn't separate in my mind three different, and seemingly unassociated, ideas that kept recurring as a monstrous, frightful trio: my gambling loss, the encounter with the tall woman, and the death of my honorable father.

"'At six o'clock sharp Major Falcón entered my study and stared at me in silence.

"'I threw myself into his arms, sobbing inconsolably, and he exclaimed as he embraced me:

"''Cry, son, cry. You need to come to grips with your grief."

IV

"My friend Telesforo," continued Gabriel after he had downed another glass of wine, "stopped for a moment upon reaching this point, and then continued as follows:

"'If my story ended here, perhaps you wouldn't find anything extraordinary or supernatural in it, and you could tell me the same thing that I was told at the time by two very commonsensical men to whom I related it—that everybody with a lively and ardent imagination has his or her own terror, that mine was solitary, nocturnal women, and that the old one on Calle de Jardines, probably a poor homeless beggar, only wanted to ask me for money when I screamed and ran away—that, or she was a repugnant bawd in a neighborhood not very virtuous in matters related to love.

"'I too wanted to believe the same thing, and I came to believe it after a few months, in spite of the fact that then I would have given years of my life to be assured of never again seeing the tall woman. On the other hand, now I would give everything I have to meet up with her one more time.'

"'To what end?'

"'To kill her on the spot!'

"'I don't understand you.'

"'You'll understand me if I tell you that I ran into her again three weeks ago, a few hours before receiving the disastrous news of the death of poor Joaquina.'

"'Tell me, tell me!'

"'There isn't all that much more. It was five o'clock in the morning and I was on my way home after spending the last night, not of love, but of bitter tears and an emotional exchange, with my former lover, the widow T———, a relationship that I had to sever, inasmuch as there had already been an announcement of my upcoming marriage to the poor thing who, unbeknownst to me, was being buried in Santa Águeda at that very hour.

"'Although daylight was not at the full, dawn was breaking on the streets that faced eastward. The lamps had just been extinguished and the night watchmen had gone off duty when, as I was about to cut across Calle del Prado, that is, go from one side of Calle del Lobo to the other, that frightful woman, that tall woman from Calle de Jardines, passed right in front of me, as if she were coming from Plaza de las Cortes and heading toward Plaza de Santa Ana.

"'She didn't look at me, and I thought she hadn't seen me. She was wearing the same clothes, and carrying the same fan, of three years ago. My fright and cowardice were greater than ever! I quickly cut across Calle del Prado as soon as she passed by, although without taking my eyes off her to be sure that she wasn't turning around. And when I reached the other side of Calle del Lobo, I took a deep breath, as if I had just swum across a rushing stream, and I again quickened my pace, but with more delight than fear, as I believed that I had bested and vanquished the hateful witch by the mere fact that I had been so close to her and she hadn't seen me.

"'But as I was approaching the house, a kind of dizzy terror gripped me all of a sudden when I wondered if the crafty old woman had indeed seen and recognized me, if she had pretended not to notice in order to let me continue down the still dark Calle del Lobo and attack me there with impunity, if she was coming up behind me, if she was already on top of me. . . .

"'And so I turned around and . . . there she was! Right behind me, practically brushing me with her clothes, looking at me with her vile eyes, showing me the repulsive gap in her teeth, fanning herself absurdly, as though she were ridiculing my childish fright.

"'I went from terror to the most senseless rage, to the savage fury of desperation, and threw myself at that awful creature. I pinned her against the wall, getting one hand on her throat, while with the other—how revolting!—I began to touch her face, her bosom, and the disgusting jumble of her gray hair until I was altogether convinced that she was indeed a human being and a woman.

"'In the meantime, she had uttered a harsh, piercing cry that struck me as false or feigned, like the hypocritical expression of a pain and fear that she didn't feel. And then, pretending to cry, but without actually crying, and looking at me with her hyenalike eyes, she asked:

"'"Why have you got it in for me?"

"'Her question increased my dread and lessened my anger.

"'"Then you remember," I shouted, "having seen me elsewhere!"

"'"I certainly do, my good sir!" she replied sardonically. "The night of San Eugenio, on Calle de Jardines, three years ago."

"'I felt cold penetrate the marrow of my bones.

"'"But who are you?" I asked without letting her go. "Why are you following me? What do you want from me?"

"'"I'm just a weak woman," she answered diabolically. "You hate and fear me for no reason. And if not, tell me, sir: why did you get scared the way you did the first time you saw me?"

"'"Because I've loathed you since the day I was born! Because you are the demon of my life!"

"'"So you've known me for a long time, have you? Well, I've known you for a long time too!"

"'"You've known me? Since when?"

"'"Since before you were born! And when I saw you pass by me three years ago, I said to myself: *He's the one!*"

"'"But who am I to you? Who are you to me?"

"'"The devil!" replied the old woman, spitting right in my face. And she eluded my grasp, running away like a blue streak with her skirts hiked above her knees, not making the slightest sound when her feet touched the ground.

"'It would have been sheer folly to try and catch her!

Besides, there were already a few people on Carrera de San Jerónimo and some on Calle del Prado too. It was broad daylight. The tall woman continued running, or flying, to Calle de las Huertas, clearly visible now in the morning sunshine, where she stopped to look back at me. Brandishing her tiny fan, she threatened me repeatedly and then disappeared around the corner. . . .

"'But wait a little longer, Gabriel, before you pass judgment on this case in which my heart and soul are at stake. Give me a few minutes more!

"'When I got home, Colonel Falcón was waiting for me. He had come to inform me that my Joaquina, my fiancée, all my hope of happiness and good fortune on earth, had died the day before in Santa Águeda! Her devastated father had telegraphed Falcón, asking him to tell me . . . me, who should have been able to *fore*tell it an hour before, upon running across the evil spirit of my life! Now do you understand why I need to kill the natural enemy of my happiness, that filthy old woman who is like a living mockery of my fate?

"'But why am I saying to kill? Is she a woman? Is she a human being? Why have I had a premonition of her since I was born? Why did she recognize me upon seeing me? Why does she turn up only when I've suffered a great misfortune? Is she Satan? Is she Death? Is she Life? Is she the Antichrist? *Who* is she? *What* is she?'"

V

"I'LL spare you the details, my dear friends," continued Gabriel, "of the reflections and arguments that I used to try to calm Telesforo, for they're the same ones, the very same ones, that all of you are preparing now to demonstrate to me that nothing supernatural or superhuman happens in my story. You'll say more: you'll say that my friend was touched in the head, that he always had been; that, at the very least, he suffered from the moral illness which some call panic reaction and others emotive delirium; that even if everything that he said about the tall woman was true, it would have to

be attributed to fortuitous coincidences of dates and circumstances; and, in short, that the poor old woman could have
been a lunatic too, or a pickpocket, or a beggar, or a bawd,
as the protagonist of my story said to himself in a moment of
lucidity and good sense."

"An admirable assumption!" exclaimed Gabriel's comrades
in different ways. "That's the very thing we were about to
suggest to you!"

"Well, listen to me awhile longer yet and you'll see that I
was wrong then, as you are wrong now. Unfortunately, the
one who was never wrong was Telesforo. Oh! It's much
easier to speak the word *madness* than to find an explanation for certain things that happen on earth."

"Tell us what you mean!"

"I'm going to, and since it's the final episode, this time I'll
pick up the thread of my story without drinking a glass of
wine first."

VI

"A few days after that conversation with Telesforo, I was
assigned to the province of Albacete* in my capacity of
forester, and not many weeks had passed when I learned,
through a public works contractor, that my unfortunate
friend had been the victim of a horrible jaundice attack. His
skin had turned completely green, he was prostrate in a
chair, couldn't work, didn't want to see anyone, wept bitterly
day and night, and the doctors had no hope whatever of
pulling him through. Then I understood why he hadn't
answered my letters. I had to resort to asking Colonel Falcón
for news of him, and each time he told me that his condition
was growing worse and worse.

"After an absence of five months, I returned to Madrid on
the same day that we received word of the battle of Tetuán.*
I remember everything as if it were yesterday. That night I
bought the indispensable *Correspondencia de España*, and
the first item I read in it was Telesforo's obituary and the
invitation to his funeral the following morning.

"It goes without saying that I not only attended the sad ceremony but went to Saint Louis Cemetery as well. I was in one of the carriages nearest the hearse, and when we arrived, an old woman caught my eye, a shabbily dressed, very tall woman who laughed irreverently as she watched the coffin being lowered. Then she positioned herself with an air of triumph in front of the gravediggers, pointing out with a tiny fan the row they needed to follow to reach the open, anxious grave.

"At the first glance, I recognized, with surprise and dread, that she was Telesforo's implacable enemy, and that she looked exactly as he had described her to me, with her enormous nose, infernal eyes, the disgusting gap in her teeth, the cotton kerchief around her head, and the tiny fan that in her hands seemed like the scepter of shamelessness and mockery.

"She noticed immediately that I was looking at her and stared at me in a strange way, as if recognizing me, as if realizing that *I* recognized *her*, as if knowing that the deceased had told me about the scenes on Calle de Jardines and Calle del Lobo, as if challenging me, as if declaring me the heir to the hatred that she had professed for my unfortunate friend.

"I confess that my fear then was greater than the astonishment caused me by those new *coincidences* or *accidents*. I saw clearly that some kind of supernatural relationship anterior to earthly life had existed between the mysterious old woman and Telesforo; but at that moment, I was concerned only about my own life, my own soul, my own happiness, which would be in danger if I were to inherit such a misfortune.

"The tall woman started to laugh and pointed at me contemptuously with her fan, as if she had read my thoughts and were betraying my cowardice to the public. I had to lean on the arm of a friend to keep from falling to the ground, and then she made a disdainful or sympathetic gesture, spun on her heels, and entered the cemetery with her head turned toward me, at once fanning herself, waving, and swaggering among the dead with a kind of infernal coquetry, until, finally, she disappeared forever in that labyrinth of plots and colonnades full of tombs.

"And I say *forever* because fifteen years have gone by and I've never seen her again. If she was a human being, she must be dead by now; and if she wasn't, I'm certain that she's scorned me.

"So . . . let's see now. Give me your opinion of such curious events. Do you still consider them *natural?*"

It would be pointless for me, the author of this story or tale that you've just read, to record here the answers given to Gabriel by his friends and comrades, since, when all is said and done, each reader shall have to judge the case according to his or her own feelings and beliefs.

I prefer, consequently, to bring this paragraph to a close, but not without extending a most affectionate and expressive greeting to five of the six companions who spent that unforgettable day together on the luxuriant heights of the Guadarrama Mountains.

Notes

Page references to this volume precede each note.

(33)   *Carrera de Darro*: a thoroughfare that runs parallel to the Darro River, at the foot of the Alhambra, the magnificent palace and grounds of the Moorish kings of Granada.

(34)   *Philip IV . . . Velázquez*: Velázquez painted many children, but perhaps the most famous of all these paintings is *Las meninas*, in Madrid's Prado Museum.

(34)   *nun . . . Saint James*: The female branch of the Order of Saint James took in the daughters of the wealthy and the nobility, and these nuns were called *comendadoras*, the feminine form of *comendador*, a high-ranking knight in one of the military orders.

(35)   *red . . . Apostle*: There are many variations of it, but almost all of them resemble a cross-shaped dagger.

(35)   *Titian's Magdalene*: Titian's [*Saint*] *Mary Magdalene* (1535) is in the Pitti Palace, Florence, and the face is indeed somewhat oval-shaped.

(36)   *War of Succession* (1701–14): The absence of a direct heir to Spain's Charles II pitted the Archduke Charles of Austria against the pro-French faction of the Spanish court, and the latter eventually won out when Charles II designated Louis XIV's grandson Philip—who would become Philip V, first of the Bourbon line in Spain—to succeed him.

(38)   *Flos Sanctorum*: a multivolume book of the lives of saints by two Jesuits, Juan Eusebio Nieremberg y Otín (1595–1658) and Francisco García (1641–85). First published in Madrid by Pedro de Rivadeneyra, early seventeenth century.

(47)   *Ataúlfo . . . Trastamara*: Ataúlfo was the first Visigothic king in Spain and occupied the throne from 410 to 415 A.D.; Don Pelayo, son of a Visigothic noble, established the kingdom of Asturias and died in 737 A.D.; [Enrique de] Trastamara ascended the throne of Castile in 1368, after killing his stepbrother Pedro I.

(47)   *Ramón María Narváez* (1800–1868): Spanish general and politician who fought in the first Carlist War and wholeheartedly embraced the cause of Queen Isabel II.

(48)   *Guipúzcoa*: a Basque province in northern Spain.

(48)   *Mondoñedo*: a city in the province of Lugo (Galicia), northwest Spain.

(48)   *fabulous potentates*: In the original Spanish, it is *preste Juan de las Indias*, or Prester John, a legendary potentate of the Middle Ages, renowned for his wealth and his kingdom.

(49)   *Puerta del Sol*: literally, the Gate of the Sun; a square in the heart of nineteenth-century Madrid.

(52)   *as Aragonese . . . father*: The Aragonese are reputed to be brave, tenacious, and stubborn.

(54)   *speaking platitudes:* In the original Spanish, it is *vicio oratorio de Pero Grullo*; Pero Grullo, an imaginary character, speaks truths that are so obvious it is foolishness to repeat them.

(56)   *Virgin . . . Zaragoza*: one of the numerous appellations of the Blessed Virgin Mary in Spain; she is venerated at Zaragoza's basilica and is the patroness of Spain; her feast day is 12 October.

(56)   *Stranger's Guidebook*: This guide originated in 1723, and by 1925 the title had changed to the *Official Guidebook of Spain*; it contains, besides an almanac, information on government officials, dignitaries, nobles, etc.

(58)   *Countess of Montijo*: Montijo is a family of the Spanish nobility that dates back to the time of Philip II (1527–98).

(58)   *General Espartero* (1793–1879): Spanish general—a great rival of Narváez—who also embraced the cause of Isabel II, fought in the first Carlist War, and became captain general of the Basque provinces.

(58)   *Convention of Vergara*: the agreement (1839) reached at the Basque [Guipúzcoa] town of Vergara between the Isabelline General Espartero and the Carlist General Maroto that put an end to the first Carlist War.

(58)   *[Rafael] Maroto* (1783–1847): Carlist general (see above) who was considered a traitor by the pretender Don Carlos for entering into negotiations to end the war.

(59)   *Carlos V*: the pretender to the throne; brother of Fernando VII, who disputed the right of the latter's daughter, Isabel II, to reign, and precipitated the three wars fought in his name.

(65)   *7 May*: On 7 May 1848 the España Regiment mutinied and took over the Plaza Mayor. It did not surrender until after hours of attack by the troops of General Narváez.

(66)   *three Marys*: a reference to the three Marys who were with Jesus at the foot of the cross: Mary his mother, Mary the wife of Clopas, and Mary Magdalene.

(68)   *velis nolis*: Latin, loosely, "like it or not."

(69)   *Riego Hymn*: the military march composed for troops who forced the tyrannical Fernando VII to swear, in 1820, to the Constitution

of 1812; the anthem of liberation; named after [General] Rafael
Riego y Núñez (1785–1823).

(69) *books of chivalry*: like *Amadís of Gaul, Tirant lo Blanc*, and—the
most famous of them all—*Don Quixote of La Mancha*, whose
protagonists epitomized the chivalric virtues of honor, valor,
piety, courtesy, and loyalty.

(73) *his father . . . Rodrigo*: which would make him Don Álvaro's
nephew, not his cousin.

(73) *civil . . . years*: a euphemistic reference to the first Carlist War,
1833–40.

(73) *tute*: a card game, not unlike pinochle, in which the object is to
win all four kings or queens.

(78) *Retiro Park*: a vast park in the heart of Madrid, replete with rose
garden, lake, crystal palace, and miles and miles of wooded
paths for strolling.

(83) *Armida*: the beautiful Saracen witch who seduces the fiery,
passionate Christian hero Rinaldo in Torquato Tasso's *Jerusalem
Delivered* (1575).

(98) *Cry . . . want!*: For the first time, in a moment of tenderness, Don
Jorge uses the familiar *tú* level of address with Angustias; he
reverts to the formal *usted* level, however, as soon as Part IV
begins.

(99) *feast . . . San Isidro*: Saint Isidore (1070–1130), a farm worker
all his life, is the patron saint of Madrid; his emblem is a sickle,
his feast day is 15 May.

(115) *Jorge! . . . there?*: For the first time, to signal her joy, Angustias
uses the familiar *tú* level of address with Don Jorge.

(115) *Etiamsi omnes*: "This chapter is titled '*Etiamsi omnes*,' the first
part of the quotation *Etiamsi omnes negaverint te, ego non* (Even
when all others deny you, I will not). This is what Peter said to
Christ in the Garden of Olives, but soon afterwards he denied
Christ three times. Similarly, the captain's fortitude did not hold
up. His avowed misogyny quickly evaporated once he met
Angustias" (DeCoster, *Pedro Antonio*, 121).

(119) *Alpujarra*: mountainous region between the provinces of Granada
and Almería, south/southeast Spain.

(119) *Mulhacén*: The Mulhacén peak in the Sierra Nevada, at an
altitude of 3,478 meters, is the highest point in the Iberian
Peninsula.

(119) *reconquered Spain*: The Reconquest [from the Moors] lasted from
718, the Battle of Covadonga, to 1492, when the Catholic king
and queen, Ferdinand and Isabel, took Granada, the Moors' last
stronghold.

(120) *Aben Humeya* (1520–68): a Moorish leader whose Christian
name was Fernando de Córdoba y Válor. He rebelled against

Philip II and started the war in the Alpujarra; he was betrayed by two of his men and strangled.

(121) *Royalists*: supporters of the absolutist king Fernando VII.

(122) *compadre*: a term used, reciprocally, by the godfather and father of a child (and, by extension, the term used by the mother and godmother of a child to refer to the godfather).

(123) *Riego . . . revolt*: See the first note for page 69.

(125) *Ceuta*: a seaport and enclave of Spain in Morocco, on the Strait of Gibraltar; located on a peninsula whose promontory forms one of the Pillars [or Gates] of Hercules.

(126) *Tarifa*: port town in the province of Cádiz, on the Strait of Gibraltar.

(126) *Anghera . . . Atlas*: The Rif Atlas range, part of the Atlas mountains in northeast Morocco, runs along the Mediterranean coast from Ceuta to Melilla.

(131) *Fez*: city in north central Morocco, due south of Ceuta.

(131) *death . . . king*: Fernando VII, in 1833.

(134) *Don . . . Austria*: Don Juan de Austria (1545–78), natural son of Emperor Carlos V; he was sent to the Alpujarra in 1569 to quell a rebellion by the subject Moors.

(139) *Oran*: city and seaport in northwest Algeria, on the Mediterranean.

(141) *sierra . . . snow*: that is, the Sierra Nevada, or "snowcovered mountain."

(153) *Don . . . Pascual*: Don Miguel Bosch y Juliá (1818–79), Don Máximo Laguna y Villanueva (1826–1902), and Don Agustín Pascual y González (?–1884), noted Spanish foresters.

(154) *San Lorenzo*: El Escorial, a town twenty-seven miles northwest of Madrid and site of the monastery, church, and mausoleum built by Philip II.

(154) *Peguerinos*: a town located on the borders of the provinces of Madrid and Segovia, on uneven terrain that forms part of the Guadarrama Mountains.

(154) *Saint . . . Louis*: The feast day of Saint James is 25 July and the feast day of Saint Louis is 25 August.

(155) *golden . . . works*: possibly a reference to the fact that between 1841 and 1862 there was considerable construction of irrigation channels, canals, highways, and—between 1854 and 1862—railroad lines.

(156) *Calle del Lobo*: in present-day Madrid, Calle de Echegaray (perpendicular to Carrera de San Jerónimo); all the other streets mentioned in this story are also real and still exist.

(157) *Despeñaperros*: the Despeñaperros gorge or pass in the provinces of Ciudad Real and Jaen; a railroad line and the main highway from Madrid to Seville pass through it; there are eight tunnels and several iron bridges.

(157) *Jaen*: Andalusian city east of Córdoba.

(158) *not . . . police*: At the time, gambling was outlawed in Spain.

(160) *Parca*: the Parcae of the Romans and the Moerae of the Greeks, the three goddesses of destiny who controlled the lives of men: Clotho, who spun the web of life; Lachesis, who measured its length; and Atropos, who cut it. Collectively called the Fates.

(167) *Albacete*: in Castilla-La Mancha, southwest of the city of Valencia.

(167) *battle of Tetuán*: 4 February 1860, in which the Spanish General Leopoldo O'Donnell defeated the Moroccans. Alarcón witnessed it and described the Spaniards' decisive victory in his *Diary of a Witness to the African War*. It was immortalized in a painting by Eduardo Rosales y Martínez (1836–73), *Batalla de Tetuán*, which is in Madrid's Museo de Arte Moderno.

Select Bibliography

First Editions of Alarcón's Short Stories and *Captain Poison*

El clavo (causa célebre). Granada: M. de Benavides, 1854.

Cuentos, artículos y novelas. Series 1ª, 2ª, y 3ª. Madrid: Imprenta de El Atalaya, 1859.

Novelas. Madrid: Durán, 1866.

Cosas que fueron. Madrid: Imprenta de La Correspondencia de España, 1871.

Amores y amoríos: historietas en prosa y verso. Madrid: A. de Carlos e hijos editores, 1875.

El Capitán Veneno. Madrid: Gaspar y Roig, 1881.

Novelas cortas, 1ª serie: Cuentos amatorios. Madrid: Imprenta y fundición de Tello, 1881. (Prepared by the author.)

Novelas cortas, 2ª serie: Historietas nacionales. Madrid: Imprenta y fundición de Tello, 1881. (Prepared by the author.)

Novelas cortas, 3ª serie: Narraciones inverosímiles. Madrid: Imprenta y fundición de Tello, 1882. (Prepared by the author.)

Twentieth-Century Collections of the Short Stories and *Captain Poison*

Dos ángeles caídos y otros escritos olvidados. Ed. Agustín Aguilar y Tejera. Madrid: Imprenta Latina, 1924.

Cuentos amatorios. Madrid: Librería General de Victoriano Suárez, 1943. Contains all the stories of the author's 1881 edition plus Mariano Catalina's biography. Text used for the translation of *The Nun*.

Historietas nacionales. Madrid: Librería General de Victoriano Suárez, 1955. Contains all the stories of the author's 1881 edition.

Narraciones inverosímiles. Madrid: Librería General de Victoriano Suárez, 1943. Contains all the stories of the author's 1882 edition. Text used for the translation of "Moors and Christians" and "The Tall Woman."

El Capitán Veneno. Madrid: Librería General de Victoriano Suárez, 1961. Text used for the translation of *Captain Poison*.

Obras completas. 3ª ed. Madrid: Fax, 1968.

Novelas completas. Madrid: Aguilar, 1974.

La comendadora, El clavo y otros cuentos [El extranjero, La mujer alta, El amigo de la muerte]. Ed. Laura de los Ríos. Madrid: Cátedra, 1975.

La mujer alta y El Capitán Veneno. Ed. Carmen Bravo-Villasante. Madrid: Mondadori España, 1988.

Cuentos. Ed. Joan Estruch. Barcelona: Ediciones Vicens-Vives, 1991. ["El carbonero alcalde," "El clavo," "La buenaventura," "El extranjero," "La mujer alta," "La comendadora," "La corneta de llaves"]

Los relatos. Ed. Mª Dolores Royo Latorre. Salamanca: Universidad de Extremadura, 1994. An admirable effort. A collection of the complete stories replete in textual variations, notes, and commentary.

English Translations of Alarcón's Short Stories Not Included in This Volume

Moors and Christians and Other Tales. Translated by Mary J. Serrano. New York: Cassell, 1891. (In addition to "Moors and Christians": "The Guardian Angel," "The Cornet," "The Orderly," "A Year in Spitzbergen," "The Gypsy's Prophecy," "A Fine Haul," "Saint and Genius," "The Account Book," and "Black Eyes.")

"The Alcalde Who Was a Charcoal-Burner." Translated by Jean Raymond Bidwell. *Living Age* 223 (1899): 514–20.

Tales from the Spanish. Translated by Mary J. Serrano, Alberta Gore Cuthbert, and George F. Duyster. Allentown: Story Classics, 1948. Translations "extensively revised and corrected" by Rafael A. Soto. (In addition to "Moors and Christians" and "The Tall Woman": "The Nail," "The Patriot Traitor" [i.e., "The French Sympathizer"], "The Cornet Player," "A Fine Haul," "The Account Book," and "The Gypsy's Prophecy.")

"A Year in Exile [Spitzbergen]." Translated by F. W. Fosa. *Golden Book* 12 (1930): 81–86.

"The Prophecy." In *Tales from the Italian and Spanish*, anon. trans. New York: Review of Reviews, 1920.

"The Stub Book." Translated by Morris Rosenblum. In *Stories from Many Lands*, edited by Morris Rosenblum. New York: Oxford, 1955.

"The French Sympathizer." Translated by Robert M. Fedorchek. *Connecticut Review* 15 (1993): 35–40.

The Nail and Other Stories. Translated by Robert M. Fedorchek. Introduction by Cyrus C. DeCoster. Lewisburg: Bucknell University Press, 1997. Contains: "The Nail," "The Cornet," "The Orderly," "The Foreigner," "The French Sympathizer," "Long Live the Pope!", "The Mayor of Lapeza," and "The Guardian Angel."

Death and the Doctor. Translated by Robert M. Fedorchek. Introduction by Lou Charnon-Deutsch. Lewisburg: Bucknell University Press, 1997. Contains: "Death's Friend."

Included in This Volume

Captain Venom/Poison. Translated by Gray Casement. Cleveland: Gardner, 1914.

The Nun. Translated by Martin Nozick. In *Great Spanish Short Stories,* edited by Angel Flores. New York: Dell Publishing Co., 1962.

Secondary Sources

Alborg, Juan Luis. *Historia de la literatura española. Realismo y naturalismo. La novela, parte primera: introducción-Fernán Caballero-Alarcón-Pereda.* Madrid: Editorial Gredos, 1996.

Azorin. *Andando y pensando.* Madrid: Espasa-Calpe, 1959.

———. *Obras selectas.* Madrid: Biblioteca Nueva, 1962. (Under "Otras páginas:" Alarcón.)

Baquero Goyanes, Mariano. *El cuento español en el siglo XIX.* Madrid: Consejo Superior de Investigaciones Científicas, 1949.

———. *El cuento español: del romanticismo al realismo.* Edición revisada por Ana L. Baquero Escudero. Madrid: Consejo Superior de Investigaciones Científicas, 1992.

Catalina, Mariano. "Biografía de don Pedro Antonio de Alarcón." In Alarcón, *Cuentos amatorios* (Librería General de Victoriano Suárez, 1943) and *Obras completas* (Fax, 1968), under Twentieth Century Collections, above.

DeCoster, Cyrus. *Pedro Antonio de Alarcón.* Boston: Twayne, 1979. (Only book-length study in English of Alarcón's life and works.)

———, ed. *Obras olvidadas [de Alarcón].* Potomac: Studia Humanitas, 1984. Madrid: Porrúa Turanzas, 1984.

Estruch, Joan. Introduction to Pedro Antonio de Alarcón, *Cuentos.* Barcelona: Ediciones Vicens-Vives, 1991.

Leguen, Brigitte. *Estructuras narrativas en los cuentos de Alarcón.* Madrid: U.N.E.D., 1988.

López, Ignacio Javier. "Humor y decoro en *El Capitán Veneno* de Pedro Antonio de Alarcón." *Boletín de la Real Academia Española* 234 (1985): 213–36.

———. "Alarcón y 'la guerra del silencio': en torno a la recepción crítica de *El Capitán Veneno*." *Insula* 46/535 (July 1991): 20–21. (Special Alarcón issue.)

Montes Huidobro, Matías. "Sencillez arquitectónica y aderezos estilísticos utilizados por Pedro Antonio de Alarcón." *Hispanófila* 34 (1968): 45–57.

Montesinos, José F. *Pedro Antonio de Alarcón*. Madrid: Editorial Castalia, 1977.

Ocano, Armando. *Alarcón*. Madrid: EPESA, 1970. (Biography.)

Pardo Bazán, Emilia. *Personajes ilustres. Pedro Antonio de Alarcón, estudio biográfico*. Madrid: La España Moderna, 1891. (Also in: *Obras completas*, III. Madrid: Aguilar, 1973.)

Pardo Canalis, Enrique. *Pedro Antonio de Alarcón*. Madrid: Compañía Bibliográfica Española, 1965.

Quinn, David. "An Ironic Reading of Pedro Antonio de Alarcón's 'La última calaverada.'" *Symposium* 31 (1977): 346–56.

Ríos, Laura de los. Introduction to Pedro Antonio de Alarcón, *La comendadora, El clavo y otros cuentos*, 11–102. 8ªed. Madrid: Cátedra, 1991.

Royo Latorre, Mª Dolores. "Alarcón en sus relatos: el problema de la originalidad creadora." *Insula* 46/535 (July 1991): 13–15. (Special Alarcón issue.)

———. "Sobre la datación alarconiana de 'La belleza ideal.'" *RILCE/Revista de filología hispánica* 8 (1992): 286–94.

———. Introduction to Pedro Antonio de Alarcón, *Los relatos*, 15–87. Salamanca: Universidad de Extremadura, 1994.

Smieja, Florian. "Pedro Antonio de Alarcón's *El extranjero*: Some Aspects of the Historical Background." *Hispanic Review* 37 (1969): 370–74.

Soria Ortega, Andrés. "Ensayo sobre Pedro Antonio de Alarcón." *Boletín de la Real Academia Española* 31 (1951): 45–92, 461–500; and 32 (1952): 119–45.

Winslow, Richard W. "The Distinction of Structure in Alarcón's *El sombrero de tres picos* and *El Capitán Veneno*." *Hispania* 46 (1963): 715–21.